Katalina

Catalyst to Murder

Scary Reading

Carolyn R Scheidies

Carolyn R. Scheidies
Author
History-Mystery-Romance
http://welcome.to/crscheidies

Other fine books by
Carolyn R. Scheidies

Thundering Heart

The Barrington Saga, Four book series

KATALINA
© 1999 by Carolyn R. Scheidies
Published by MountainView Publishing
A division of Treble Heart Books
July 1, 2001
http://www.trebleheartbooks.com

This book was originally published by
Heartsong Presents—Barbour Publishing.

This is a revised, expanded version.
© copyright 2002 by Carolyn R. Scheidies

Cover Design
© copyright 2002 by Lee Emory
All rights reserved

ISBN: 1-928602-15-0

DEDICATION

This book is dedicated to a very real orthopedic surgeon and friend, Dr. Ken Ellis, who got me up and walking.

This book is also dedicated to my other fine orthopedic surgeons:

Dr. Brent Adamson
Dr. Gordon Walker
Dr. Kevin Garvin
THANKS!!

Other than Dr. Ellis, all characters in the book are fictional.

DISCLAIMER

The background of this story is drawn from my own rich Swedish heritage, but the tangled family relationships come solely from my imagination.

KATALINA

CATALYST FOR MURDER

CAROLYN R. SCHIEDIES

MOUNTAINVIEW PUBLISHING A DIVISION OF TREBLE HEART BOOKS

PROLOGUE

Hearing a boom of thunder, Kit Anderson stared out the box-like window of her small apartment as raindrops tapped on the pane and dripped to the empty flower box beneath the window.

Though she loved flowers, she hadn't had the energy to plant anything. Maybe next year when she was stronger and walked with more sureness, she'd plant chrysanthemums and roses.

Absently, she tried to massage the dull ache from her leg. Usually she sensed the weather changes long before the rain or snow actually hit, but not today. Was she healing, or was her mind simply clouded with the memories of the death of her parents? They had been too young to die, one after the other, as though they couldn't endure separation. The day heralded an anniversary of sorts, of her father's death. She disliked the anniversary, disliked remembering, disliked knowing she was alone.

The muggy air clung about her in the darkened room, and she sucked in a long shuddering breath. *Lord, are you there? Do you really care?*

Memories assailed her, memories of a dark and frightening rehabilitation center. Things had happened there, and even now she tried to shut them out of her mind because they made her feel vulnerable and worthless. They made her wonder about God's care.

The phone's *brring* against the lightning flash, followed by a thunderous crash, sent an eerie chill up her spine.

For a moment, Kit stared at the phone before reaching out a hesitant hand to pick up the ivory handset. "Hello?"

Rain splattered on the windowpane as though seeking a way through the glass. Kit turned her back against the sudden deluge.

"Hello, is anyone there?" she asked into the crackling earpiece.

"Kit, is that you?"

"Yes." She strained to hear the disembodied voice on the other end.

"Kit, it's your Aunt Augusta."

Kit's shoulders slumped in relief. She tried to still an irrepressible giggle. Who was she expecting, the boogey-man? "Auntie, how are you?"

Her aunt's voice faded in and out. "Wait, Auntie, I think we have a bad connection. Let me try another phone."

Away from the window, thought Kit. *Away from the storm.*

Laying down the phone, she headed into the bedroom that was carefully arranged to give her plenty of room to move about freely. Fumbling with the drapery pull, Kit finally managed to close the drapes against the fury of the storm.

Picking up the receiver of her blue phone, she asked her aunt to wait while she hung up the other line. Unable to hear her aunt's response, she hoped Augusta understood.

Hurrying back into the kitchen-dining room combination, she hung up the receiver and returned to the bedroom. Sitting on the edge of the thick midnight- blue comforter, she took up the phone. "Is this better?"

To her relief, her aunt's voice came through clearly. "Kit." Her voice shook. "I'm so glad I caught you at home. I tried last night and...."

"I was at church, Aunt Augusta."

"Yes...yes, of course." Her tall, gaunt aunt sounded even more hesitant than usual.

"Are you all right, Auntie?" Kit's lips pursed in concern. When her aunt didn't answer, she asked more sharply. "Aunt Augusta?"

"Kit, oh Kit...something awful has happened.... "

CHAPTER ONE

Finally, my brethren, be strong in the Lord, and in the power of His might. Eph.6:10 (KJV)

Behind the large wooden desk that took up most of his small but plush office in his new orthopedic clinic, Dr. Ken Ellis sat back in his deep cushioned chair. Absently, he tapped long, dexterous fingers on the desk mat in front of him. Behind tan glasses his eyes narrowed with concern as he surveyed with affection the elfin young woman seated in the blue velvet chair opposite him.

Her wide eyes, the dark blue of a stormy summer day, held his steadily. Her small, pointed chin, raised in stubborn resolve, indicated she had already made up her mind as to her course of action. He knew nothing short of force would keep her from doing as she wished. Her crooked fingers tightly grasped the arms of her overstuffed chair. Her petite body leaned slightly forward in her desire to persuade him. Recognizing the signs, he stilled the frown tugging the corners of his mouth.

"I don't like it, Kit. You've just gotten off your crutches. This is no time to go gallivanting off to Minneapolis by yourself. Minneapolis, Kit, like in big city. We're not talking home town, not talking Kearney, Nebraska, you know." He paused significantly. "I understand your desire to help and to be with your mother's family during this time, but this...sche...ah, plan of yours...."

"Hare-brained scheme, you mean," supplied Kit.

He was having more difficulty keeping his demeanor stern. "Well, isn't it? No one need tell me how strong your will is, Kit Anderson, but up to now you've always shown at least a modicum of common sense."

Kit's eyes narrowed. "Are you saying this makes no sense?"

"Does it? Think about it. You're heading off to the city with no idea of what barriers await you."

Though her face paled, Kit's eyes remained steady. "Aunt Augusta needs me."

Dr. Ellis actually grunted. "Maybe so, but this is about your capabilities right now. Think it through, Kit. How do you plan on getting on and off at least two different airplanes? How will you manage to get about in large terminals without completely exhausting yourself? And, what would happen if you fell?"

Kit grimaced at the word picture. She felt herself weaken...and hated herself for her weakness.

Dr. Ellis didn't have to remind her of the four years she spent in reconstructive surgery to repair damage done by the Rheumatoid Arthritis she acquired at the age of thirteen. She might still have the disease today, if her father had not taken her to those revival meetings in Texas where a little known evangelist prayed over her. While the pain disappeared instantly, her fingers remained just as gnarled and her legs just as bent as ever.

Kit remembered the months she struggled with her faith after this partial healing. In time she reached the conclusion that God hadn't completely healed her because she had failed him in some fundamental way. Maybe she didn't have enough faith.

She glanced down at her hands, which were a vivid reminder of her failure as both a person and a Christian. Or, had God failed her? In the last two years he took away both her mother and father, one through a stroke and the other through a heart attack. Her parents died within a few months of each other. The double whammy spun her into a depression from which she was only now emerging.

Four years ago, locked in a wheelchair, she made the acquaintance of Dr. Ellis. The families became friends and Kit came to trust this doctor. So many others made promises to get her up and walking; so many others failed. Ellis made no such promise.

His wry comment stuck with her. "I can't make you any worse."

It made sense. Sealed into dependence by a wheelchair she was unable to wheel herself, Kit was ready to make one last grab at independence.

No one told her it would be so difficult.

It took four years of surgery to reconstruct her legs and to get her back on her feet. These included a new set of knees and a new set of hips, as well as innumerable other surgeries. It took almost another year to relearn how to walk...if you could call those first toddling steps walking...before she could discard the crutches. Dr. Ellis couldn't promise she wouldn't need more surgery in the future.

No wonder her doctor hesitated about giving his approval. To be honest, that's exactly what Kit sought, the doctor's approval...as well as his advice. Instead he questioned her decision.

Kit wanted to lash out against the doctor who had become her friend. During those long months of recovery he listened to her frustrations and continued to encourage her. After the death of her parents, he'd helped her find an apartment with one of the office nurses who had also been Kit's friend all through college. Kit knew why he paired her up with a nurse. Though Kit hated to admit it, she still needed assistance now and again. Thankfully, Ruth looked after her without being obtrusive.

Kit's dependence haunted her. She wanted to be able to fend for herself, wanted a life outside of doctors and hospitals. Now she had the chance to prove her capabilities.

Gramma Clara wanted her to come to Minneapolis, and Aunt Augusta had all but begged her not to ignore the old woman's summons.

"She's dying, Katalina," Augusta choked out when she called. "She's dying. You must not disappoint her. You're all she has left now of Sophia. Your mother cannot come. You must." The hesitation so a much a part of the tall, gaunt woman's makeup, surfaced. "Pl...please come, Katalina. You will come? I'll be glad to reimburse you for your plane fare. I know this is an imposition, but..."

"Aunt Augusta, I want to come, but I...I...yes I *will* come."

Her shoulder's rigid, Kit determined not to fidget before the doctor's penetrating gaze. "I have to go," she asserted. "There's no one else, no one else but me to go. Gramma Clara asked for *me*! How can I disappoint her? Surely God can take care of me, can't he?" She threw out the gambit hoping to convince the doctor. Instead of questioning her decision, why couldn't Ellis help her?

Getting to his feet, the doctor paced back and forth in the small space behind his desk. Turning, he glanced up at the cabinets and shelves built into the walls behind the desk. For a moment he stared at a picture of his wife, Carolyn, and their three children. His gaze seemed to focus on the picture of his daughter.

"I don't like it. How are you going to climb into the plane? What about changing planes? Just how are you going to do this without assistance?" His eyes narrowed and he tugged on his white coat. "Is there someone who would go with you? They shouldn't have to pay full fare, you know."

Kit shook her head. Her shoulders slumped. "No one. I tried. I was hoping you'd have a suggestion along that line."

When he remained silent, she grew defensive. "I know the problems, but I have to go. One way or another, I *am* going."

"Kit, your determination served you very well when you fought to relearn to walk after being confined to a wheelchair for ten years. But..." His eyes darkened with concern. "But, your determination is both your best friend and your worst enemy."

After a long pause, Kit could almost see the light go on in his head. Swinging around, he punched a button on the multi-line phone on his desk. "Send in Dr. Long," he barked into the receiver.

Now what? "What are you doing?" Kit let go the arms of the chair to clench her hands in her lap. Why had Ellis called in Dr. Long? If it had been one of the other orthopedic doctors she could understand, but Dr. Long? Wasn't he the newly hired psychologist?

As the newest staff member at the Kearney Orthopedic Clinic, Dr. Long was another step in Dr. Ellis' dream for a clinic where all of the doctors professed Christ. But what did this have to do with her?

Kit bit her lip to keep her curiosity at bay. Silence reigned in the office while they waited. The doctor's slight smile told her he understood. In his presence, Kit felt like a child instead of a young woman quickly growing into maturity. Did one always feel like this with the friends of one's parents, or did she feel like this because in many ways the doctor had taken on a parenting role after the death of her parents? It bore thinking about...later.

Some five minutes later the door opened, admitting perhaps the tallest man, with the exception of maybe a basketball player, Kit had ever seen. Dr. Long's head brushed the top of the doorframe filled by his broad shoulders. Absently he pushed away the thatch of rich dark brown hair spilling over his wide forehead into his unfathomable gray eyes.

"You wanted to see me, Ken?" His tone held respect, and why not? Dr. Ellis was one of the best orthopedic doctors in the Midwest.

Kit felt herself shrink into the oversized chair as Dr. Long's gaze flashed over her dismissingly, before he turned his gaze toward the compact doctor. Indicating another chair, Ellis sat down behind his desk as though the large desk would give him the same overwhelming sense of presence the taller man had just by entering the room.

"Dr. Long, I want you to meet a patient of mine. Katalina Anderson. Kit."

"Miss Anderson." Dr. Long nodded toward her. His penetrating gaze seemed to pierce to the very core of her being.

Kit managed a smile. *His discomforting gaze must come from his being a "shrink."*

"How do you do, Dr. Long," she said, turning puzzled eyes toward her doctor.

Leaning back in his chair, Ellis surveyed the two young people who waited for him to speak. "Dr. Long, I know you have a conference in Minneapolis. When do you plan to leave?"

Tensing, Kit turned her gaze on the tall psychologist. "Monday morning." He wasted no words, but his single lifted eyebrow spoke volumes. The gesture reminded Kit sharply of Mr. Spock on the original Star Trek episodes, as did his rather taciturn expression.

Dr. Ellis nodded. "You're flying out Monday morning." Looking rather smug, he glanced toward Kit. "Good enough. I understand you plan to stay with your sister and family in the Minneapolis area rather than at the conference site itself. You will be able to come and go as you please, right?"

Dr. Long answered carefully, as though aware Ken had reasons for asking questions to which he already knew the answers. "Um, yes, that's right. There isn't a problem is there? This time off was understood when I accepted the position here at the clinic."

"Of course." Ellis rubbed his hands. "But I do have a little problem you might help me solve, Keith."

Dr. Long's enigmatic face gave no hint he realized, as did Kit, Ken's use of his first name put this on a personal, rather than on a professional level. From the lift of his eyebrow and the sudden tightening of his face, Kit sensed the tall psychologist wondered just what the good doctor had in mind. "I'm listening."

Ellis cleared his throat. "You may have heard me speak of Miss Anderson here."

Kit felt Dr. Long's gaze on her in a long, slow evaluation. At his impersonal examination, color inched up into her cheeks. "I have." His eyebrow lifted.

As though understanding his associate's methods, Ellis waited a moment before continuing. Dr. Long's slow and silent evaluation made Kit fidget. She could almost swear she saw Keith's pointed ears.

Keith Long watched the color stain the young woman's pale cheeks, then drain away, leaving her paler than ever. Her reaction sparked his interest. Few young women these days blushed. Usually they lost that innocent little gesture before they left grade school...*or even kindergarten*, he thought cynically.

Her impossibly long, dark lashes brushed her too pale cheeks as though she was recovering from a long illness. He frowned. From what he recalled, she was. Keith felt her instinctive withdrawal from his silent scrutiny. He also recalled hearing her case discussed and remembered the girl was more than just another patient to Ken. He remembered little else. It didn't matter.

"Kit has a problem," Ken said. "Her grandmother, who may be dying, has asked her to come to Minneapolis to stay with her. However..." Dr. Ellis clasped his hands, and leaned forward slightly in his chair. "Kit...Miss Anderson...is as yet unable to travel alone."

"I haven't tried," broke in Kit. Color rose in her cheeks once more. "I am not about to..."

Ellis went on as though she had not interrupted. "Keith, I have no intention of giving her my permission to go unless she has someone along willing to look out for her—both there and back."

"I'm of age," Kit retorted. "Besides, I don't know how long I'm staying."

Keith glanced her way. From the way she glared back at him, he knew she read surprise in his eyes. He watched the anger and frustration vie for supremacy in the young woman's face. Looking at her, he found it difficult to believe this young woman with her oval face, clear guileless eyes and sensitive lips, was anything more than an innocent, vulnerable child.

"And you want me to chaperone the young lady." It was not a question. Playing chaperone was the last thing, well, almost the last thing he wished to do on his trip.

"Exactly." No doubt Ken sensed his train of thought. It seemed to make no difference. "I'm sure you two will get along real well." A glint of humor sparkled in Ellis' eyes. "I'm sure you can keep Miss Anderson well in hand. I suspect she'll behave better for you than for me."

Kit went crimson at her doctor's chuckle. An angry retort strangled in her throat. There had always been somewhat of a friendly war of words between her and Dr. Ellis, but would Dr.

Long understand? For some unexplained reason, Kit wanted the tall psychologist to think the best of her. But from the look on his cold, distant face, she'd already failed. The thought left her strangely depressed.

Biting her lip, she glared down at her hands as though they offended her. Maybe they did. Had she not been crippled, she wouldn't be submitting herself to this humiliation. Obviously Dr. Long wanted no part of Dr. Ellis' goofy scheme. Fat chance he'd put himself out for someone like her; not that she blamed him.

For a moment, Kit glanced at Dr. Long's rugged handsome face. *The man has probably never had a sick day in his life. Surely he'll nix Dr. Ellis' idea of personally escorting me to the Twin Cities. Probably be embarrassed to be seen with the likes of me.*

She envisioned the tall, blond, sophisticated women who undoubtedly graced his arm in the evenings. Kit's conscience scolded her. *He's a Christian Kit, or Dr. Ellis wouldn't have hired him to work at the clinic.*

Kit surveyed the enigmatic man. Dr. Long must be a good man...and trustworthy. Otherwise Dr. Ellis wouldn't recommend, or *coerce* him into helping her. She caught Dr. Long watching her and felt the crimson creep back into her cheeks.

With a laconic smile, he drawled, "If Miss Anderson can put up with me, I guess I can do the same." He waited for her reluctant nod. "Will that solve your little problem, Ken?"

This time her doctor grinned. "It sure will...and thanks. I owe you."

"Good. I'll have my secretary make her reservations."

He turned to Kit. "Miss Anderson, Kit, if I may...I don't suppose you drive?"

She clenched her teeth at the amusement in his eyes when she swelled up indignantly. "Of course I do!"

"Good enough. I won't need to pick you up Monday. I'll see you at the airport, say about eleven."

"I'll be there, Dr. Long, if you're sure you want a 'little problem' like me along." Immediately she flushed, wishing she could take back her hasty words.

Dr. Long's eyes narrowed. "I'm sure," he said, "you won't present much more than that."

Her humiliation complete, he took his leave. As Ellis chuckled, she wished the floor would open and swallow her whole.

CHAPTER TWO

"Fear thou not; for I am with thee: be not dismayed; for I am thy God: I will strengthen thee; yea I will help thee: yea I will uphold thee with the right hand of my righteousness." Isaiah 41:10

Keith surveyed the young woman on his right as she gazed out the small airplane window. Not for the first time, he wondered what possessed him to agree to accompany Kit Anderson to the Twin Cities. Obviously she had little desire for a chaperone, and even less for his company. Nervously she twisted a narrow gold bracelet on her thin wrist.

Her gesture was not lost on him. It was the same one she used when he found her waiting in the small airport terminal. After a long night with a particularly difficult patient who'd had to be admitted to Richard Young for long term psychological treatment, he forgot to set his alarm. Only the sharp bark of the neighbor's dog woke him. His irritation at being jarred awake, again, by the huge black lab quickly turned to gratitude when he glanced at his clock.

Reminding himself to buy the big, friendly mutt a steak on his return, Keith threw off the covers and lunged to his feet. Still groggy, he threw off his pajama bottoms as he headed for the shower. The steamy, needle-sharp water pounded him awake. He liked his showers hot, and his showerhead set on massage. This morning he needed it.

Stepping from the shower, he quickly toweled dry, brushed his hair, shaved, and headed to his closet. After a swift perusal of his clothes, he picked out a navy suit with a pastel blue shirt. It was quick, easy...and it was business-like. Precisely the image he wished to present at the conference.

As he sifted through the ties on the rack, he realized he'd packed his conservative ties. For a moment, just a moment, he turned toward his suitcase ready to go on the floor by the door. *Thank you, Lord, that I packed yesterday afternoon!*

No! Forget that. With a grin, Keith picked out a tie with a picture of Mr. Spock posing in front of the Enterprise spread across the width. Throwing it around his neck, he tucked the tie beneath his jacket. The tie was his own petty rebellion.

No time for breakfast, Keith grabbed his suitcase along with his laptop, and locked the door to the three-bedroom house he'd been fortunate to purchase on the north side of town. A modernized version of a Federal style house, complete with tall pillars over the front entry, the residence was surrounded by carefully trimmed trees and bushes that edged a huge, fenced-in back yard. It was a yard meant for children. Someday, when he met the right woman, it'd be perfect. He smiled, but as he glanced at his watch the smile faded into a grimace.

Roaring out of the driveway, he made it to the airport with minutes to spare. *All right*, he conceded, *minutes*, if he counted how late the plane landed.

He found Kit waiting in the terminal, her head turned toward the doors and her eyes wide with anxiety. At his nod her shoulders eased, but her frown remained. He checked in and waited for her, only to realize she needed assistance even with the small amount of luggage she'd brought along.

Stilling his impatience, Keith checked her in as well, made provisions for their luggage, and escorted her to the plane. Boarding the plane posed another problem. Her cheeks blazed with embarrassment as she slowly moved up the steep steps, one after another. Her breath grew ragged and labored long before she reached the door of the plane, but she didn't complain.

Keith sensed the impatience of the attendants and the others waiting to board. Let them wait. Kit probably knew exactly what a traffic jam she caused; yet she continued on bravely. Her smile of triumph as she reached the top step, blazed with such brilliance it wiped the frown off the face of the attractive attendant. With a smile, she quickly showed them to their first class seats where Kit had plenty of room to stretch out her legs.

"Have you flown before?" he asked.

"No." Kit glanced toward the window. "But I'm looking forward to it."

"Then take the window seat. You'll see better."

Her smile did something to his insides. "Thanks." Her soft musical tones pulled a close second.

Trying to shake off the feelings she evoked in him, Keith watched the graceful movements of the attendant as he sat down with his laptop on his lap. It was small and efficient, and he never left home without it. Kit eyed the computer with something akin to envy. Keith didn't invite her comments, and she offered none.

Since she mentioned she'd never flown before, he assumed Kit, who appeared so fragile, might well be frightened. Instead, the roar of the engines and the impact of the lift-off brought a grin to her pale face. She had a nice smile. Once aloft, her soft "ahh's" as she surveyed the miniature landscape below, made him chuckle. She didn't even hear him and, for some reason, that rankled.

His yawn drew her attention. "Tired?"

"Some."

"Up late last night? Me, too. I was so excited, and..."

"Worried," he said.

She nodded. "All right, yes, worried. I didn't sleep much either." This time she yawned and lay back against the cushioned seat. He sensed he made her nervous. She confirmed it when she once more twisted her bracelet.

"Is your bracelet special?"

Kit gulped, glanced toward him then away, before answering. Before she turned, he glimpsed a shimmer of tears. "My, ah, father gave it to me on my last birthday. It was my last one with him. And...it was after...after mom died."

"I'm sorry."

Shrugging, Kit pushed the long brunette braid from her shoulder. Inadvertently she brushed against her companion's arm.

Keith felt her stiffen and lean away. "I'm not going to bite," he drawled.

She flushed, but her embarrassment quickly turned to irritation. "I'm well aware of that." When she glanced up at him, he noticed her large blue eyes were fringed with the longest natural lashes he'd ever seen.

While she stared out the window at her side, Kit's gnarled fingers clutched and unclenched the slender purse hanging at her side. Keith had the strangest feeling she didn't want to look him in the face. Her behavior both baffled and intrigued him.

Let the little minx keep to herself. What do I care? Feeling rather grumpy, Keith wondered why her behavior bothered him. After all, he was just doing a favor for a friend.

Surreptitiously he glanced over her petite figure, from the slender waist; high bust; narrow shoulders; small, oval face; long, lustrous hair; and sweetly curved lips, to those delightfully telling eyes. The innocence of that face made him shake his head. He had difficulty believing the young lady more than sixteen, rather than the twenty-one she professed. In a world of jaded beauty queens, she was a throw back to a more innocent time—when innocence was a virtue...not a defect.

Could Kit really be as innocent as her wide eyes and open smile indicated? If so, he'd need to take care she was protected. Now where did that thought come from? He really must have his head examined. Once he made sure Kit got to her grandmother's house, he'd wipe his hands of her until they traveled back to Kearney together. That was the sum total of his involvement. It's all Ken asked, and it was all the time he planned to offer.

With that, Keith repositioned his laptop and flipped it open. At least she wasn't striking up a conversation. He never could abide a person who chatted on nonsensically while expecting him to listen to every syllable. Clicking on his program, Keith glanced toward his charge.

Her shoulders tense, Kit stared out the window. Good. She seemed disinclined to flatter him with some overrated feminine wiles. She wouldn't get very far if she did.

Long ago he quite logically determined what qualities he sought in the woman he would one day ask to be his wife. For sure little Miss Anderson did not qualify. *Not that she angled for the position*.

Over the years, he got in the habit of measuring every woman he met by his list of standards. Automatically, he ticked off his requirements as he studied the young woman at his side.

First of all she was much too short. Her head barely touched his heart. She was light as a feather when he helped her up the steep steps to the plane.

That was another requirement he had not considered, but it made sense. He certainly did not envision his wife as disabled in any way.

Kit's "problems" didn't bother him. Quite the contrary, he told himself hastily. Actually he thought she carried herself very well. In fact, Kit almost made one forget she was disabled...until she needed an arm to assist her on the stairs, or down a curb.

Secondly, though she spoke without the vulgarity so prevalent in young women these days, she didn't have the sophistication he required in the wife of an up and coming psychologist.

Thirdly, not only wasn't she blond, she didn't have the desired voluptuous figure. Besides, she looked so young and innocent. Her deep blue eyes seem to mirror her every thought. Finding her gaze on him; he started. "K...Kit," he stumbled over her name at being caught staring.

"Why do you always gawk at me as though I'm some freak?" As she nervously smoothed down the leg of her blue slacks, her gaze challenged him.

"Maybe I'm just trying to figure you out, Miss Anderson." He felt like a little boy caught with his hand in the forbidden cookie jar. He didn't much like the feeling.

She smiled then, and her face transformed into sunshine. "I'm not an imbecile, Dr. Long. If you want to know something, ask." Her soft mobile lips turned up in a teasing grin, and forced a reluctant smile to Keith's face.

"Ah, I see you can smile."

At that he closed his laptop. *The minx was going to open up to him, after all. That could be interesting. This was the reason he had agreed to baby-sit Kit.* Plane trips could be excruciatingly boring. The cynical smile that twisted his lips, he directed toward himself.

"Now your smile isn't so nice," Kit told him. "Do you enjoy frightening people in general, or just me?"

An eyebrow rose. "Do I frighten you?"

"Ah Mr. Spock with your reserved expression and penetrating gaze, you not only intimidate by your size, but by the way you look at me. It's as though you can read my thoughts." Kit smiled a tight, thin smile. "That's somewhat disconcerting. Since I don't suppose you're Vulcan, I can only suppose that 'look' comes with the job."

At this, Keith smiled a smile that actually reached his eyes. "Maybe so. Are you always so forthright?"

Kit shrugged. "I try to be. I *am* sorry Dr. Ellis conned you into this bit of baby-sitting. I know it's rather a bother."

"I could have refused."

Kit grinned. "Sure you could have, and Dr. Ellis would have thought you a jerk."

"You have me there." He paused, thoughtful. "Do you always put yourself down as you did just now?"

"What, put myself down?"

"Yes, do you always think of yourself as a bother, a problem? Or is this just for my benefit?"

Anger deepened the color in Kit's cheeks. "You made it quite clear before we left that you considered me nothing more than a problem. I'm a *little problem* to be handled, nothing more."

"The phrase was your own, you recall." Keith's eyes narrowed. The girl was sharp. He liked that.

"You echoed it."

A slender smile played at the corners of Keith's mouth. He was enjoying sparring with her. "That didn't answer my question."

"I'm hardly anything but a problem," Kit retorted. Tears stung her eyes. Not wanting the psychologist to see how much his calm but penetrating words affected her, Kit turned away from him.

Below her the earth stretched like an earth model. Tiny toy-like trains chugged along on toothpick tracks. Blue, red, yellow and white cars vied for rights to the narrow, black ribbon road. Farm fields spread out below the shadow of the plane like little chessboard squares, albeit green and brown rather than regulation red and black.

Like the fields below, Kit felt her own security slipping away. It was, she thought, more than leaving behind her home, her friends. In the presence of the enigmatic psychologist, turbulent new emotions whirled inside her; confusing, bewildering feelings for which she had no name. He angered and intrigued her, frightened her, yet drew her trust.

Kit sensed Dr. Long watching her profile and knew he could all but see the conflicting emotions flitting across her transparent face. "Kit. Kit look at me."

Determined not to let him boss her around, Kit stubbornly raised her chin. As he softened his tone and dropped the note of command, she turned. Catching the slow smile, so characteristic of the man, she couldn't help smiling in return. Her stomach twisted into a thousand knots. That slightly cynical smile devastated her.

A flush warmed her cheeks at the sudden memory of the warmth of his arms when he'd helped her aboard. Drat him anyway! Would she ever stop blushing like some child at her every thought of this arrogant man? She felt so young and inexperienced. Well, wasn't she? She'd never had so much as a single date.

So here she was acting like an idiot over her reluctant chaperone who was only doing her doctor a favor. How she must look to him with her crippled hands and decided limp. She found herself wanting to hide them. This thought surprised her. Had she even yet not accepted herself as she was? She knew the answer to that question.

She hated being disabled, hated being different, not being able to take care of herself, always having to depend on the largess of others. She knew now she would never be a whole person. She was a failure. How often had she seen the instinctive revulsion in the eyes of those to whom she was being introduced, and felt the light touch on her hand rather than a firm handshake? At least Dr. Long hadn't rejected her. Casting him a sidelong glance, she wondered why.

"Kit," Dr. Long repeated, seemingly amused by her stubbornness. "I'd like to be your friend." Her eyes widened in surprise. "Well?"

"You...truly...wish to be my friend?"

"Does that surprise you so much?"

She nodded.

"You're a lovely young woman, Kit. Anyone would be privileged to know you."

Her features hardened even while he spoke.

"It's true," he added.

"You just don't know. I know how people look at me, like I'm some circus show freak."

"As you accused me...wrongly."

"I'm sorry." Kit's face grew warm, then she smiled at him shyly. "I'd like to be your friend. Does that mean I'm no longer your little problem, Dr. Long?"

Dr. Long threw back his head and laughed. "You win. And, since we're going to be friends, how about calling me by my first name...Keith."

Kit stumbled over the name. "How about Spock instead?"

With that he pulled out his tie. At his wry grin, Kit giggled. "Spock it is."

By the time their plane landed in Omaha, the two conversed like the friends they'd become. Besides Star Trek, both found many other interests in common. They enjoyed their sparring immensely, with neither one giving an inch in their opinion of those interests. Keith was surprised at how swiftly the hour had virtually "flown by."

It took some doing to get Kit off the plane. Tired, she allowed him to carry her, though she seemed to find it difficult to relax in his arms. He caught her grimace as he set her down on the other side of the gate. "You all right?"

"Don't worry. It always takes me a minute to steady myself." Though she smiled, her fingers clutched his arm until she felt secure. He waited until she released him.

"Ready?" When she nodded, he took his laptop from the flight attendant who had carried it out for him. His eyes followed her as she walked away. As they reached the building, he glanced down to find Kit rolling her eyes.

"Lov...e...ly, I'm sure," she mimicked, lifting her nose.

"Minx," he growled, as he took her arm. "I missed breakfast and I'm hungry. How about a bite to eat?"

"I didn't miss breakfast," she teased.

"So where is that growl coming from?"

"My stomach is not..." At his grin, she said, "You got me. Truth? I am getting hungry. I was too..."

"Worried."

"All right, too worried to eat much."

"Good. Let's go then."

Giving her no time to answer, Keith steered her inside the long terminal. Once inside he strode down the long hallway, halting only when he heard Kit's labored breathing beside him. "Sorry. I didn't think."

Stopping, Kit leaned against the wall. "It's...all...right. Th...anks...for...sto...pping."

After giving her time to catch her breath, he slowed his long steps to hers. When they reached the booth of an eating establishment inside the large building, it didn't surprise him when she took out two painkillers and popped them in her mouth.

"Sorry. Maybe I should have asked for a wheelchair," he said.

Kit tensed. "No way. I don't want to use a wheelchair. Hopefully, I'll never need one again."

Keith's eyes narrowed at her vehemence.

"Oh, stop analyzing me."

"All right." He stilled the grin threatening to spread across his lips. The grin, he was certain, would further irritate, if not insult his traveling companion. "However, I *am* interested in knowing what you meant by that peculiar look you threw me when I insisted on carrying you from the plane."

Glancing down at the almost empty glass of water in her hand, Kit nervously swirled the liquid. "I could have gone down those stairs myself...with some help. I also knew it would take forever. I was trying to decide which would be more embarrassing for you, helping me down or carrying me. I knew carrying me would end your misery quickly."

His eyebrow rose. "You were thinking of me...not yourself?"

Kit shrugged. "I'm used to it."

At that moment, a waitress with shoulder-length, dark hair strode over to the table. Holding her pencil over a small tablet, she sighed. "Well, what'll it be?"

Without consulting Kit, Keith ordered a large dinner for each of them. Kit's face whitened. He waited until the waitress left their table before asking, "What is it Kit?" When she hesitated, he said, "We're friends, right? Friends aren't afraid to tell the truth to each other."

Swallowing, Kit tried make light of the situation. Her strained smile told another story. "I'm afraid the plane ticket took most of my, admittedly, meager savings."

"And...?" Keith encouraged her to continue.

"Ooooh. All right. My part time job as a stringer for the local newspaper scarcely keeps me in necessities. I hadn't planned to eat much on the flight."

"The meal I ordered will make more of a dent than you'd prefer in your cash reserves, right? I take it you're traveling on the proverbial shoestring. But," Keith said, lifting an expressive eyebrow, "since I ordered without your consent, there's little you can do about that now. Right?"

Again Kit shrugged, her eyes on her glass. Red stained her cheeks.

Laying a large hand over hers, Keith reassured her. "I intended for you to be my guest," he told her firmly. "As for the other...Let me assure you, I was in no way embarrassed. I've always taken the viewpoint that one need not be embarrassed, nor apologize for those things which are unavoidable."

Something akin to hope sprang to life deep in Kit. "I never thought of it like that. Just because of my, ah, limitations, I know I embarrass some people when I'm around them. They either don't know what to do, or what to say. Sometimes I can alleviate it just by talking to them. Other times...." She blinked quickly. She wouldn't cry. She wouldn't!

It disturbed her that, on such short acquaintance, she exposed her deepest thoughts and feelings to this man...this virtual stranger. That certainly was unusual. Even with Dr. Ellis, whom she liked and trusted, she seldom shared anything deeper than her medical problems. Maybe sharing came easily with Keith because inner feelings were his expertise. Still, something about him drew her. He seemed to understand, but how could he?

Her heartbeat quickened when he touched her half-fisted hand, his eyes dark with concern. "Don't let this dictate who you are, Kit. You're a child of God, of the King of Kings and Lord of Lords. All of His children are worthy of love and respect. Even if no one else gives it to you, respect yourself. You'll find others will, too. What's important is who you are inside. And, Kit Anderson, I have a feeling the Kit you keep hidden because she fears being hurt again, is a young woman well worth knowing."

Kit gaped, her eyes wide. "How...how can you know this?" It was as though he'd entered her mind and laid bare her deepest fears. Her hand trembled when his grasp tightened. With effort, she kept herself from grasping his hand in return. She wanted him as a friend, and right now he was a lifeline of hope. *Did she also want him as a...?* Kit refused to let her mind even consider a third reason why she might be grasping his hand, why she felt drawn to him. And it wouldn't do to even consider for a moment that Keith might be drawn to her. No way!

Of course, she told herself, counseling was Keith's vocation, probably because he could empathize. He knew; somehow he knew! Every word he spoke rang true. His softened voice flowed over her caressingly. "Don't cocoon yourself from fear, Kit. Barriers not only protect, they also keep out those who care about you. Don't let fear stop you from reaching out to others, Kit."

As he gazed into her troubled face, something sparked between them; something far removed from the clattering sound of dishes, the clinking of glassware, and the drone of conversations at other tables. Kit swallowed as a warm glow puddled somewhere in her middle. In another second she'd embarrass both of them by blurting out something totally inane.

Thankfully, at that moment, the waitress arrived with their plates and Keith released her hand. It tingled from his touch. Kit felt she'd lost something precious, something...She was losing her mind.

Grabbing up her fork, she studiously attacked her steak—a steak she never would have ordered for herself. The last thing she wanted Keith to know was that her wrists were weak. To her immense relief, the sharp steak knife sliced easily through the tender cut.

It embarrassed her to sit sawing at a tough piece of meat, unable to either cut or eat it. It didn't even need to be all that tough for it to defeat her weak efforts to slice it. This, however, cut like a dream and melted deliciously in her mouth.

***

Keith watched the delight in Kit's eyes with growing affection. He could understand Dr. Ellis' paternalistic affection for this woman who found such delight in simple pleasures. Her musical laughter danced in his mind and her smile lifted his spirits. There had been something when they touched.... Shaking his head, he studied Kit for a moment longer, before reminding himself she didn't even begin to meet his criteria. Then again.... *No!* He shied away from the thought.

All too soon it was time to return to the plane and lift off for the last leg of the trip. Kit found it difficult to keep her eyes open, but each time her head drifted it hit the window ledge and startled her awake. Indulgently, and to Kit's embarrassment, Keith put a long arm around her shoulders. With his other hand, he pulled her head against his shoulder.

Kit tensed. He smelled invitingly of musk and his low chuckle rumbled through her. "Relax, Kit. I promise I don't bite."

"I know that." The man was dangerous. Did he know how he affected her? She fervently hoped not. He might be too large for her taste, but otherwise he was the epitome of her dream.

I really must stop this, she scolded herself silently. She tried to force herself to move away from his arms, but he held her fast.

"Go to sleep, Kit. I know you're tired." Keith's low deep voice soothed her. She *was* tired. "Relax now...relax."

Slowly she relaxed against his chest, a soft smile on her soft lips. Moments later she slept.

***

Smiling boyishly, he watched her sleep. And against all reason, he warmed to the feel of her slight form cuddled against him.

CHAPTER THREE

I can do all things through Christ which strengtheth me.
Philippians 4:13

Kit awoke slowly, drowsily. She felt warm and secure in the circle of Keith's arm. She made no move to disentangle herself. Instead she let her mind wander aimlessly ahead to Minneapolis, to the small house where Gramma Clara and her Aunt Augusta anxiously awaited her arrival.

If her mother, Sophia, had been still alive, it would be she who flew to the side of her stepmother. Kit had always seen her mother as capable, always calm in a crisis, but her mother was gone and now Aunt Augusta would have to rely on her niece's inadequate resources.

Kit tried to determine what bothered her so much about the phone call. Aunt Augusta sounded nervous when she called, but then she always did. She seemed so strange on the phone, but then her aunt had always been a bit...well, peculiar. She'd sounded...frightened. She'd covered it well, but Kit heard the undertone of fear.

She'd begged Kit to honor her mother's dying request, a request that made little sense to Kit. Why had her aunt asked her to bring along the flat, polished mahogany jewelry box that had belonged to Kit's mother, and her mother before her?

Why did Gramma Clara want to see the box?

Kit recalled stroking the cool surface of the box the night her mother collapsed and died of a massive cerebral hemorrhage. She closed her eyes at the painful memory. Her mother cherished the jewelry box with its worn red velvet interior. Kit cherished it as well. Just having it in her possession gave her the feeling of roots stretching back in time and space.

"This jewelry box," her mother once told her, "has been in my family for several generations."

Now it belonged to Kit. Gramma Clara was not Sophia's real mother, but her stepmother. The box had not been in *her* family! Why would she request the jewelry box? Surely she wasn't planning to take it away from Kit.

As Kit shook her head slightly against the warmth of Keith's shoulder, the texture of his suit jacket brushed against the softness of her skin. If letting Gramma have the box made her happy, why not give it to her? It still belonged to Kit.

Shuddering, the plane settled into a landing pattern over the large, sprawling city. Yawning, Kit sat up. She blushed at the amused light in Keith's eyes as he removed his arm. "Feel better now?"

"Much. Thanks," Kit said, trying to distance herself from his all-too-tempting embrace. As she moved away, the plane jerked, throwing her against him once again. Almost automatically, his arms enclosed her. She felt so warm and safe and secure. Marshaling her runaway thoughts, she pushed away. For a moment Keith's arms held her. Their faces mere inches apart, his gaze fell on her lips. If she tilted her head just so....

This time Keith set her upright...away from him. Mortified, Kit stuttered, "Th...thanks again."

Keith chuckled, a low, deep chuckle ascending from somewhere deep in his large chest. "My pleasure, Miss...Kit."

Scolding herself silently for her moment of weakness, Kit stared out the window at her side. Had she really thought he wanted to kiss her? How ridiculous could one person be! Hadn't she learned her lesson long ago when not even well-meaning friends could find someone willing to ask her out? With a shudder, she recalled the polite smiles and hesitant handshakes. Handshakes on a date! Never again, she told herself.

Yet here she was, getting all wide-eyed over a handsome stranger. Yes, she reminded herself, *a stranger*. However much he seemed to know her heart, the man who traveled beside her was a stranger. Worse, he was her *baby-sitter*, at the request of her doctor.

The memory drained the warmth from her recent encounters with Dr. Long. He only did his "Christian" duty. Once he dropped her off, she'd probably not see him again until they flew back. That was just fine with her! She lied. Glaring out the window, she dashed a tear from her eye as she forced herself to concentrate on what was happening outside the window.

Before long, the city stretched out below them far into the distance. Gasping, Kit stared as the buildings, cars, and people grew more and more life-like and less like toys. The sound of the massive engines thundered in her ears. Opening her mouth wide, she tried to get her ears to pop.

Gazing down at the city she had not seen in seven years, Kit remembered her father driving her here. She hadn't wanted to come. She hadn't wanted to go to a rehabilitation center for treatment. In fact, she'd tried to talk her folks into letting her design her own treatment, at home, in the security of her family. They hadn't listened.

She remembered how small she felt in the undersized wheelchair she couldn't push by herself. Still, the time spent here had been good for her. She'd made new friends and learned how to use what capabilities she had to dress herself with certain dressing aids, even comb her hair and pull on her socks. It hadn't helped her walk again though, which had been as great a disappointment to her mother and father as it had been to her.

Dr. Ellis, right in Kearney, had changed that. Her father always said God led them to Kearney not for a job, but that she could meet Dr. Ellis. Maybe he was right. He usually was. But her father was gone. He was gone when she needed him most. *Why, God? Why?*

Pushing her questions aside to more practical matters, Kit tried to stretch her legs. Would she be able to stand after being in such a cramped space for so long? She rubbed the knee of her pant leg, feeling the long scar underneath. It matched the scar on the other knee. There were also scars under her legs and on her hips. They itched.

Nevertheless, she relished the straightness of her legs even though they were far from perfect. The weeks of painful surgery and the months of therapy were worth the ability to walk again, however imperfectly. God *had* answered her prayer to walk again. Things would have been so much worse had she still been tied to a wheelchair.

Suddenly an inner joy bubbled up inside at being alive.

As her smile faded, Keith asked, "What's wrong?"

"I'm alive, but Gramma Clara—" Kit twisted the gold band on her arm. "Poor Gramma Clara...and poor Aunt Augusta."

She sighed and suddenly panicked. "I wonder who's going to pick me up?"

"Doesn't your aunt drive?"

Kit shook her head. "Never did. I hope they remember to send someone."

Keith squeezed her hand and, Kit noted with amazement, there was neither rejection nor revulsion in his firm touch. "Don't worry. I'll see you get to your grandmother's house. I shan't let the wolf get you." He smiled and Kit smiled back at his reference to Little Red Riding Hood.

The plane landed and smoothly taxied to a stop. Reaching over, Keith unbuckled Kit's seat belt. He smiled to himself cynically, already beginning to anticipate her needs. Not being a particularly sensitive man, this anticipation made him wonder at himself. He liked watching the blush on her delicate cheekbones, and the way she pursed those delightfully soft, red lips.

Whoa!

To his chagrin, he'd almost kissed her earlier and he wasn't about to make that mistake again. What sort of man would she think he was if he took advantage of her vulnerability? What was the matter with him anyway?

Kit affected him in ways he never would have predicted. If he had, he would have found some way, any way, to excuse himself from his promise to Ken. *She's not my type*, he reminded himself again. She wasn't? No, of course not. He shook his head. For his own peace of mind, he needed to get her safely settled and focus on the conference.

The flight attendant, seeing Keith about to help Kit to her feet, quickly moved to his side. "Please wait," she said. "It will be easier if you wait until the others have deplaned."

Though Keith frowned with annoyance, Kit sat back with a sigh of relief. She seemed only too glad to have her departure witnessed by as few persons as possible. The other passengers hastened down the aisle in orderly fashion. A middle-aged merchant whose paunch pushed through his open suit coat, filed past, followed by a thin, well-tailored business professional. After him, strode a matronly woman with carefully arranged hair carrying a dark leather briefcase, and a nervous older lady who smiled as she passed Kit. Most of the passengers nodded and hurriedly moved on. Beside her Keith shifted impatiently, his eyes on the door.

Finally the shapely stewardess returned. "You can leave now. May I help you, miss?"

Unfolding his long legs, Keith stood, bumped his head on the ceiling, grunted, and ducked down again. "Thank you, but she's in my charge."

"Anything I can do?" Surveying the accommodating stewardess, Keith couldn't help noticing the long legs and nicely rounded figure. To his irritation, Kit intercepted his survey with a knowing smile on her lips. Unfortunately the smile wasn't reflected in her eyes. In some way, he knew he'd hurt her and didn't like how that made him feel. Maybe that was the trouble. This little waif of a woman confused him, irritated him, and muddled his thinking. He didn't want to feel like that. He was a man of logic and reason...as was his faith.

Turning away from those large eyes, Keith thrust his laptop into her capable hands. "If you'd hang onto this, I'd appreciate it."

Taking the diminutive hand Kit held out to him, he pulled her to her feet. For a moment Kit swayed, her body stiff from sitting in the same position too long. Automatically, Keith's hands spanned her waist to steady her.

She blushed. "Sorry. It takes me awhile to get balanced and moving again."

Maybe she did confuse him, but it was his Christian duty to help her. He grinned. Besides, she felt so right snuggled against his side.

When she stumbled, his grin widened and he held her, if anything, more firmly. "It's perfectly all right, m'lady." He nodded formally, but his tone was gently teasing.

Despite Kit's pronounced blush, he continued to hold her as she gingerly took a step forward, then two. With each step she grew more confident as her joints seemed to limbered up.

At the narrow doorway, she glanced down apprehensively at the steep, narrow steps rolled against the plane. A moment later she gasped when Keith grinned, picked her up and lightly descended the stairs. He didn't set her down until they were inside the building.

As he set her on her feet, the stewardess held up the laptop case. "Your case, Dr. Long." She smiled at him with bright, straight teeth, as her gaze swept over him appreciatively. "I'm laying over a couple of days," she tendered.

"I'm sure you'll enjoy the rest," Keith said indifferently. He glanced at Kit, who was biting her lip to keep from giggling.

The stewardess's eyes flashed. "Yes, I'm sure I will." She took her leave politely enough, but with a particularly angry flounce to her hips as she marched away.

"She's a bit put out with you," Kit commented.

"No reason she should be."

"Don't tell me you didn't notice her?"

Keith glanced down at Kit. A smile quirked his mouth. Funny how she managed to coax a smile from him. "I noticed. She's not my type."

Kit stared up at him in disbelief. "I thought she was every man's type. At least," she hastened to add, "so I've heard. In the plane I thought..."

Kit's naiveté overcame his irritation. "There are considerations other than a well developed body, Miss Anderson." He couldn't bring himself to use the stern scolding tone he intended, especially since her innocent observation held more than a hint of truth. He was beginning to understand why Ken had not wanted her running around without supervision in a large city. Ken would never have left Kit in his care had he known how she could affect him...or would he?

Keith's own words, however, startled him as he recalled his carefully considered requirements in which the figure of his future wife played a prominent part. He cleared his throat. "I suppose we need to see if you have a ride."

"Yes. I sure hope I do." Her eyes held hesitation and fear.

***

A person who highly valued honesty, Kit knew she lied. Feeling out of place in the city, she didn't want Keith to leave her alone. Not yet. After all her talk about coming to Minneapolis on her own, she found Ken's reservations all too real. How foolish she'd been! She couldn't have gotten anywhere without Keith.

It amazed her that in such a short span of time she could feel so close to a person. She'd confided more in him in the last few hours than in any number of friends she'd known for years. With them it seemed she always held back, afraid to reach out. But Keith did this sort of thing for a living. No wonder she felt comfortable talking to him. If only her heart wouldn't go into overdrive whenever he touched her. If only she didn't want to feel those strong arms around her once again. If only....

"Katalina. Katalina Anderson."

Kit glanced about for the person who called her name. "Yes?"

"*You're* Katalina Anderson?"

Cringing at the insulting tone, Kit stared up into the haughtiest, coldest blue eyes she'd ever seen. "Yes, I'm Katalina."

The middle-aged man glaring down at her with his washed out eyes, sent a chill down her spine. "Lars. Lars Bergstrom." Nodding, he added sarcastically, "Your *d-e-a-r* aunt sent me to pick you up."

"Glad to meet you, Lars." Inwardly she groaned, and mentally added another lie to her account. She wasn't in the least glad to see this man with the reddened nose and large paunch on his rather small frame, whom she knew only by reputation. Gramma Clara thought him a ner-do-well. From what she'd heard, he'd never held a steady job. She hated to admit any relationship with her cousin-once-removed. Thankfully, he wasn't really even that—a step-cousin, actually.

Instantly contrite, Kit scolded herself silently for her quick judgment. "Lars, this is Dr. Long who..." She stumbled as to how to explain his presence.

Keith extended a large hand, taking Lars' weakly proffered one in return. "Since I had a conference in town, we thought it would be nice to keep each other company on the trip." His lips twitched in amusement.

Catching his gaze, Kit smiled back her gratitude.

"So you've come to pick her up?" Keith asked Lars.

Lars nodded. "Where's your stuff? I wanta get going."

Keith frowned at the man's brusque tone. "Kit, if I may, let me take your suitcase to the car."

Again she was grateful and flashed him another smile.

Ignoring both his cousin and the psychologist, Lars strode ahead of them with ill-conceived grace. Thankfully, Keith paced his strides to hers so that Lars, whose strides usually would have been no match for those of Dr. Long, quickly outdistanced them. Vainly, Kit tried to keep up. Her sides ached with the effort.

All around her, sounds hemmed her in: the clanging of metal against metal, raised voices, the roar of planes taking off and landing. The noises echoed unpleasantly in Kit's ears until she wanted to cover them. Her head pounded with the sounds she had forgotten. How she hated the continuous discordant sounds of the city.

She grimaced as much from the pain of the raucous din as from her shortness of breath. Keith took her arm to steady her as she stood heaving, catching her breath painfully at the baggage counter. Thankfully both her and Keith's luggage arrived safely. Kit had scarcely caught her breath before Lars whipped away from the counter and strode down the long hall to his car.

Keith, holding both his own two cases, and Kit's small suitcase, followed. He tried to juggle his laptop case as well, but Kit took it from him. "Let me take that." She bristled with anger at her cousin's deliberate rudeness.

Lars turned, an impatient frown on his face, and waited for them to catch up. As they neared, he took off again. Minutes after he headed out a side door, they followed. Outside, he already had his dusty, well-worn Escort revving. He didn't so much as lean over to open the door.

Keith hoped his anger wasn't evident to Kit. He hesitated a moment before setting down his luggage to put her case on the back seat. Opening the front door, he waited for her to slide onto a seat that hadn't seen a decent cleaning in years. Dust clung to the handle, the dash, and obscured the mirror. He almost pulled Kit out to take her himself, but thought better of it. After all, Lars was her cousin and had been sent to pick her up.

As she settled into the dusty interior, she handed him his laptop. "Better not forget this...Spock." Though Kit spoke lightly, teasingly, her eyes mirrored her anxiety.

"I'll call," he assured her. "What's the name again?"

"Kit." A smile played at the corners of her mouth.

With her attempt to lighten the moment, his admiration grew. Though obviously fearful, she hung onto both her self-control and her dignity. "Not yours, your Grandmother's."

Kit gave it to him and, as he closed the door, he touched her cheek reassuringly. Their gazes met and held. "Don't worry," he said. Absently stroking down her cheek, he wished there was something more he could say or do.

Through the open window, he leaned down to address Lars. "Nice to meet you, Mr. Bergstrom." Impatiently Lars mumbled a reply, revving the engine as he did so.

Standing bareheaded on the hot pavement, Keith watched as Kit and her less-than-gentlemanly cousin roared away. For some indefinable reason, he felt he'd let her down. Maybe he had. Maybe he had at that.

***

Watching over her shoulder until Keith disappeared from sight, Kit felt humiliated by her cousin's actions. Why had Aunt Augusta sent *him,* of all people? She wished Keith could have brought her to her grandmother's house, but that would have made her just that much more of a burden to him. Kit sighed.

Out of the corner of her eye she surveyed her cousin. He looked more than twice Keith's age. *Probably,* she thought, *it came from years of indulgent living.*

"Wondering where I fit in, huh? I don't fit the pretty family picture, right?" He looked at her instead of at the road.

Kit shrugged. "No, you don't."

Her forthrightness startled him. "Don't remember me then?"

When she didn't answer, he said, "I'm Edmund's son."

"Yes, I remember. Edmund is Gramma Clara's brother. I've heard about you, but I don't remember ever meeting you."

"Don't matter," Lars sneered. "The family has little enough to do with me."

Kit changed the subject. "How is Gramma?"

"Old lady's holding her own. Too stubborn to kick off, I guess." Lars rolled his tongue with relish. "But when she croaks, all her precious silver and the rest of her estate goes to her next of kin. They may not like it, but that includes yours truly."

Kit studied Lars' hard-set features. His body, behind the wheel, thrust forward threateningly. She shuddered at his callousness.

Gulping back her apprehension, she asked in a voice she hoped didn't tremble, "And your father, how is he?"

"Weak as always. With Clara at death's door, so to speak, all the old man does is sit in the corner of her living room in her favorite chair and turn a dumb hourglass over and over. Drives me bats."

"He's worried about his sister, because he loves her."

Lars grunted. Was it a swallowed laugh? Kit couldn't be sure.

"Well, why'd you come?" he asked.

"I came to see Gramma, before...you know."

"Just bet you did." The sneer returned. "What you trying to get out of the old lady?"

"Nothing! I think you're being unduly nasty."

Lars laughed. "Spunky! Didn't think it of you since you...since you're...." He gestured toward her hands. "But words don't mean nothin'. Gramma Clara hardly knows you."

Kit's stomach burned with suppressed anger. "Maybe not, but that doesn't mean I don't care about her. She's my grandmother after all. I came because she asked for me. Wouldn't you come?"

"Step-grandmother," Lars corrected, ignoring her question. "Besides, the old lady is too sick to ask you to come." He sounded suspicious. "Why would she ask you to come and stay when her own brother and nephew have to live elsewhere?"

"Gramma only has two bedrooms." Kit shook her head at her cousin's insensitivity. "And it was Aunt Augusta who called me. But Gramma Clara *did* ask her to send for me." Kit was certain it was her mother who her grandmother really wanted to see. She sighed and blinked away the tears stinging her eyes, determined not to cry in front of her cousin.

"Why would she want ta see you?"

"Why not ask her?"

This time Lars shuddered. "I'm not about to go anywhere near that pasty-faced old lady."

Kit gasped. "She's your aunt! Don't you care about her at all?"

Lars growled, "Ain't no help for her now. Why should I go in to see her? She never cared much for me."

"Understandable," Kit muttered under her breath. Certainly Lars was not one of the family's shining specimens of manhood.

He interrupted her thoughts. "If that old woman is trying to cut us out of her will...." Kit heard his threat.

"Before you threaten me, are you so sure you're even in Gramma Clara's will?" Kit asked.

"I'd better be," Lars told her. "At any rate, no cripple's going to do me out of what's mine."

Kit stared at her cousin with disgust. "I have no idea what Gramma Clara has in her will...or even if she has one! And I have no idea why she asked me to come to Minneapolis except that I, too, am family."

Pushing her damp bangs back from her forehead, Kit glanced toward Lars. "Besides, I think Aunt Augusta should get almost everything. She's the one who's stayed with Gramma all these years."

Lars snorted. "You mean Clara has been taking care of *her* all these years."

Afraid that if she said any thing more she would begin to rage at this nasty, unfeeling excuse for a relative, Kit turned away.

On the way to his room, Keith compared the bright cleanliness of the taxi with Kit's transportation. He wished he had gone with his inclination to send Lars on his way without Kit. He couldn't get her anxious face from his mind. Something about that cousin of hers bothered him.

He shook himself. He had a conference to attend. Later, he'd check on Kit. Later.

CHAPTER FOUR

She lieth in wait as for a prey, and increaseth the transgressors among men. Proverbs 23:28

Kit sighed thankfully as Lars pulled off the freeway onto the avenue lined with tall green oak and maple trees, that stood as sentinels to the medium-sized houses in the quiet neighborhood. It amazed Kit now as it did years ago, how even in a large city such small-town neighborhoods still existed.

Lars whizzed passed an assortment of brick and painted homes surrounded by lawns, several of which needed cutting. Window boxes blazed with a profusion of colorful flowers while hedges, though tall enough for privacy, were cut low enough for a neighborly chat.

Suddenly a gray and white cat sauntered across the street. Lars made no effort to slow down. If anything, he appeared to speed up.

"Slow down. Don't you see the cat?"

"Serve her right to get hit," he growled.

Kit's eyes widened. "Slow down, Lars." It was a command.

Lars jerked his head to stare at Kit's tight-lipped frown. Throwing a rude comment in her direction, he nonetheless slowed. He missed, by inches, the cat that realized her danger and leaped toward the side.

Aching with exhaustion, and tired of Lars' behavior and his remarks, Kit leaned forward. Hoping to recognize something familiar that would tell her the uncomfortable ride would soon be over, she almost missed the small white house among the slightly larger white, blue, and yellow houses surrounding it on the quiet street.

The mellow two-story house showed her aunt's predilection for perfection in the neat English cottage appearance of siding, trim, and shutters. In front, the bushes were trimmed to perfection, the grass recently cut, and the sidewalk, unlike that in front of many of the other homes on the street, was smooth and free of cracks and weeds.

Seeing Kit's appreciation of the well-kept lot, Lars commented sarcastically, "Now that Pop isn't well enough to help Augusta with the house and lawn, she actually expects me to help her. Can you see *me* on my hands and knees digging up weeds!"

Kit glanced at the soft white hands resting on the steering wheel. "No, I certainly can not. But I also don't see why you can't help out."

"Why should I? Let her hire someone to help. It's not as though she's ready for the poorhouse."

Shaking her head in disgust, Kit struggled with her growing dislike for this self-centered cousin. It was hopeless to talk to the man. A few minutes later, as frustration welled up inside her, she decided "selfish" was not near a strong enough word for the greedy, grasping man.

Carelessly parking the car along the curb, Lars shut off the motor, grabbed his keys, and exited to the house leaving Kit gaping after him in astonishment.

"Of all the low down...." Kit stared at her cousin's retreating figure. "Lars!" He didn't even turn around. Anger simmered, then faded as Kit leaned against the seat. For the first time since getting into the car, she relaxed. She was here. *Thank you, Lord.*

Staring at the door, Kit visualized the two-story bungalow. She remembered that while the downstairs was both comfortable and welcoming, the second floor had never been finished and remained just one large storage room under the eaves.

The main floor held a large dining room, cozy living room, and a tiny kitchen on the far side of the dining room, two bedrooms and a bath off the short hallway leading from the dining room. As Kit surveyed the house and tried to decide what to do, she wondered if anyone peered at her from the curtained windows. *Curtained?* It was strange they remained closed in the middle of the afternoon.

Kit visualized her aunt's fluttering concern when she didn't follow in her cousin's wake, but no one appeared to realize she sat alone in the car. Fleetingly she wished for Keith's strong arms to assist her, but she was on her own this time. Hadn't she insisted to Dr. Ellis she was capable of taking care of herself? Now she'd have to prove it.

Guess it's up to me, Lord, and I need help.

Tentatively, she jammed her curled fingers around the short handle and prayed she wouldn't get them stuck between the handle and the door. She'd done that before. Even now she felt her cheeks warm with the remembrance. More often, she didn't have the strength in her wrist to pull the handle hard enough to release the door latch. Faced with the prospect of languishing in the hot, muggy car alone, Kit closed her eyes as she tugged on the handle.

Help me, Lord. Please help me open the door. Finally, her fingers aching, Kit gave one long hard jerk. Though she wrenched her wrist, the door swung open.

"Thank you, Lord," Kit said, glancing upward. "Thanks." Kicking the door wide open, she swung out her legs and stood up. Precariously she kept a hand on the car as she heaved herself up onto the curb. Smiling at her accomplishment, Kit stretched her aching limbs before taking a couple of tentative steps. Turning, she pushed the door closed. The movement unbalanced her and, for a moment, she teetered back and forth. *Lord, help me!*

Gulping, she caught herself and limped up the sidewalk to the house. Eyeing the steps, she gingerly touched the wrought iron railing. Good. It felt solid! Kit surprised herself by negotiating the shallow steps quite easily.

So far, so good...no thanks to Lars. Reaching the screen door, Kit breathed a prayer of thankfulness for Keith's care on the plane trip. Only now was she was beginning to truly appreciate him. Just knowing he, too, was in Minneapolis gave her a feeling of security. He promised to call. Would he? Her heartbeat quickened. Oh, she hoped so.

Not bothering with the doorbell, Kit, thankful both doors opened easily, walked into the house. As she emerged from the bright sunlight, the darkened room shocked her. Why were the blinds down and the curtains drawn in the middle of the afternoon?

Blinking in the semi-darkness, Kit's eyes slowly adjusted to the image of Lars lounging on the well-kept couch that was covered in a muted flowered-patterned material. He grinned up at her sardonically. "See ya finally made it into the house."

Regarding his slovenly figure with a coolness she didn't feel, Kit retorted, "No thanks to you! Why didn't you stay and help me?"

"You made it on your own, didn't you?"

"And if I hadn't?"

His eyes raked her petite figure. Even in the dim room Kit read revulsion in his eyes. "Don't expect pampering around here. This ain't no nursing home." The implication was clear.

Absently, Kit rubbed the wrist she'd twisted when opening the car door. His manner infuriated her and she gritted her teeth to keep from saying something she'd regret.

As though sensing her restraint, Lars grinned at her with malicious delight. "What, nothing to say? Can't figure out why you got invited here. It's not as though Clara needs someone else to take care of her. It's not as though you'd be of any help anyway. Jest another mouth to feed."

His assessment coincided all to closely with her own, and her face flushed. All set to snap back at him, she stopped when a faint movement in the corner caught her eyes.

Stepping further into the room, Kit squinted at the white, shrunken little person in the corner. A thin shaft of sunlight fell across his face, making his eyes seem to glisten menacingly.

"Uncle Edmund!" exclaimed Kit. How he'd changed!

The shrunken man's head bobbed stiffly. His eyes glinted eerily.

"Uncle Edmund, why is it so dark in here? It's broad daylight. Here, let me open the curtains."

"No!" At the crackling voice, Kit started.

"My dear father doesn't care for light, do ya Dad?" Lars mocked his father with an undertone Kit didn't understand.

Kit shook her head. This couldn't be real. Had she landed in a circus fun house, or maybe some kind of a nightmare? "I don't understand. It's the middle of the day. It's dark in here. Why don't you want me to open the curtains?"

When neither occupant answered her, she cleared her throat. "Where's Aunt Augusta?"

A large, cheery woman with a round face strode heavily into the room. "Your aunt is still at work. She'll be home around five, five thirty, depending on traffic. Buses often get caught in it for hours." Smiling she stuck out her large, callused hand. "Oh, I'm Sally Callen, Clara's private nurse. And you're Katalina."

"Kit." Hesitantly she held out her hand, and was gratified to find it enveloped warmly and firmly. Her smile widened. "Nice to meet you, Ms Callen." She paused. "How is Gramma? May I see her, Ms. Callen?"

"Sally, dearie. Everyone calls me Sally. And, I'm afraid you'll have to wait to see your grandmother. She's sleeping right now." The matronly nurse threw a malevolent glare toward the other two occupants of the room. "You just come on into the kitchen with me where the curtains *are* open. I have some hot water on. Will you join me?"

"Thanks, Sally. I'd like that." Kit wondered if the woman heard the relief so evident in her tone. Probably, for Sally threw her an enigmatic smile before leading the way through the dining room to the kitchen. Thankful to leave behind the oppressive gloom of the living room, Kit followed.

Sitting on a stool beside the small kitchen table along the wall, Kit relaxed in the homey kitchen. Not much had changed here in seven years except for maybe a new coat of paint. Sunlight pouring through the window reflected off of the blue and yellow Swedish decor and affirmed the change from the murky living room. Gauze curtains, even closed, would have done little to hold out the light.

Sally, bustling purposefully about the kitchen, reminded Kit of her mother. Expecting the usual steaming cup of thick, rich coffee, Kit was surprised when Sally asked, "I'm having tea. Do you prefer coffee like most Swedes?"

Kit shook her head. "Tea's fine. Afraid I never developed a taste for coffee. Actually I prefer herb teas when I can get them."

Sally's capable hands set two Blue Wedgwood cups on the table and added a tea bag to each, then poured bubbling water into the cups. "Sugar?" she asked, settling her large frame into the deceptively fragile kitchen chairs.

"No thanks." Kit snuggled her hands around the cup; at least as much as her curled fingers would allow. The warmth felt good even in the muggy heat of the afternoon. "Besides, it'll be sometime before this cools down to my tolerance level." She watched Sally spoon sugar into her tea. "Does Uncle Edmund ever do more than sit in that chair? Lars says that's about all he does."

Sally snorted. "As though Lars does much more. Those two. Gloomy pair aren't they?"

"Lars certainly wasn't the friendliest on the drive here."

"He never is," said Sally. "I don't think even Edmund cares much for him, and Lars is his own son."

Kit's eyes darkened in compassion. "If his own father doesn't care about him, no wonder Lars is the way he is. He's so...so surly. Has he always been like that?"

"Who knows? Probably doesn't even know himself. He doesn't have the brains. When he disappeared for several years, no one knew where he'd gotten to."

Kit heard an implied *or cared,* and it saddened her. "Why did he return home?"

"Guess he heard about Clara and came back. He's been useful in running errands and doing odd jobs around the place, and doing other things as well."

"Like picking me up."

"Yes, that's right. Like picking you up."

"He doesn't care much for yard work."

"Or work in general," Sally said with a decidedly sarcastic snort. "As for being surly, he's been pretty much the same for as long as I've known him, and I was around while he was growing up. He's worse now, though. Usually he and Edmund do nothing but wait in that dark living room like a couple of vultures."

"Lars wants Gramma to die. He's already making plans for his part of the estate. Can you believe he thinks I came here just to steal his part of the inheritance?" Kit sniffed. "As though I'd rip off my own gramma."

Sally's eyes narrowed. "Do you know how much your grandmother might leave? Or to whom?"

Kit shrugged. "She's not wealthy, but she does have lots of

china, some quite valuable silver tea sets, oak chests, furniture, and all the linen she has either made or embroidered. I don't know. Isn't the house already in Aunt Augusta's name?"

"True enough." Sally sipped her tea before asking, "Lars say anything else?"

"Not really. I'm sure Gramma left both Lars and Uncle Edmund something, but Augusta has been the one who's been taking care of her all these years. She should get most everything."

Sally smiled at Kit over the rim of her cup. "Your visit is a surprise, you know. Why *did* you come?"

At Kit's pained expression, Sally patted her hand. "Don't worry, I'm not going to accuse you of gold digging."

Blinking rapidly, Kit set down her teacup. "Actually, Gramma asked for me."

Her eyes on Kit, Sally took another long sip. "Did she say why?"

"I'm the closest she can come to my mother."

Reaching across the table, Sally again patted Kit's hand. "I'm sorry about your mother." Tears stung Kit's eyes at the woman's unexpected gesture. "I see you have your mother's sensitivity," Sally said.

"You knew Mom well?" Hopeful, Kit searched Sally's face.

"Yes, I knew her before that dashing, young minister swept her off her feet, married her and carried her off to parts far away. We lost contact over the years. Now, I'm delighted to meet her daughter. Dearie, you remind me of her. Though you have your father's large deep blue eyes, you have your mother's ready smile. You haven't her plump figure. You must have gotten your petite figure from your father. He was so wiry."

"I suppose I did. Food did tend to stay on Mother's bones."

Sally patted her own ample bosom. "Like it does on mine." They laughed together.

"Oh, Sally, after that dreadful ride with Lars, it's such a relief to meet you. Are you here often?"

"I'm afraid I spend most of my time here, now that Clara needs constant attention."

"Are you here at night, too?"

"Oh, no. I have an apartment on Nicolette. Besides, Augusta keeps pretty close watch on her mother when she's home."

"How long has Gramma needed a nurse?"

"For some months now. But, dearie, though I lost touch with Sophia, your aunt and I have been friends right along. When Clara needed a nurse, Augusta naturally turned to me. Seems I've been helping out the family in one way or another for years."

Kit finished her tea. "Hard to see the two of you as friends. You seem so different from one another. Aunt Augusta is...well...unsure, and you're so confident."

Sally's chin shook as she laughed. "She's a perfectionist, and I'm just the opposite. She went to finishing school, because your family always did have money. I did housekeeping for the family to pay for my nurse's training."

"So Aunt Augusta ended up at IDS as the president's executive secretary, and you a nurse. Speaking for myself, I find the latter the more important position."

"Maybe so," Sally told her, "but through the years the elegant Augusta has earned perks through her job, including a good chunk of prime stock. Not to mention she had the prestige of working in the IDS tower, once the tallest building in Minneapolis. A nurse, on the other hand, moves from one job to another, without so much as a thank you half the time."

Kit thought she heard a note of jealousy in Sally's voice, but when she glanced at her face it was as pleasant and as unlined as ever. Kit turned her teacup around and around between her fingers. "I have a hard time seeing Augusta as the decisive secretary when she is anything but that here at home.

"When she used to visit us," Kit smiled at the memory of her indecisive aunt's behavior, "she'd drive Mom to distraction, because she could *never* make her mind up about anything! She couldn't even decide whether to take a bus or plane home, which forced my mother and father to make the decision for her."

"For all that," Kit continued, "she has stuck by Gramma Clara all these years. Since Gramma's gotten sick, that must have been a heavy burden."

"Dearie, she 'stuck around' as you say because she couldn't decide whether to marry or not. She had some pretty good offers too, I tell you. I'd have snatched them up in a second. She was just too timid to take the chance."

"Mama said once that she thought, for some reason, Aunt Augusta was afraid any man she married would die and leave her stranded and alone. She didn't want to risk that pain. And when Mama died, Aunt Augusta went to pieces. She talked to me after the funeral and she was terrified. Even though they didn't live close to each other, somehow Aunt Augusta clung to her emotionally. Maybe it was because Mama was the older sister."

"Half sister," corrected Sally, rather too quickly.

"Well, with Gramma Clara dying, I can imagine what Aunt Augusta is going through now."

"Aye, poor Augusta." Sally finished off her tea and poured herself another cup.

"I can understand some of her fear. I admit the thought of flying to Minneapolis alone was scary. But I did it." Kit smiled gently as she thought of Keith's protective concern.

"Left behind someone special?" guessed Sally.

Kit blushed. "No. No. Nothing like that." She stared down at her fingers despondently. "I have lots of friends, but...no one special. Who'd want to be stuck with someone like me for life?"

"A petite thing like you? Why I'll bet there's a host of guys out there who'd overlook your, umm, limitations. Men seem to go for the pretty face and slender form. Now with me...." The woman patted her ambled middle.

Clearing her throat, Kit changed the subject. "Are you married?"

"Afraid not. Came close only once." She looked down at her bulk. "Not many relish this type of figure." She laughed ruefully.

"Or my disability. I can't see anyone loving me as I am. Still, God has been good to me." Kit grinned. "At least I can walk."

"I can see. I know Clara has followed your progress. She appreciated the letters first your mother, then you wrote. But there is something different now. Clara has something on her mind." Sally frowned. "She may be dying, but her mind's as sharp as it ever was. Not like Edmund."

She snorted her disgust. "Maybe...maybe you can find out what's bothering your grandmother." She hesitated, then added, "You know dearie, it would be such a help to her if you could relieve her mind of whatever it is that's troubling her. So if you find out anything..."

Kit nodded. She already knew Gramma had something on her mind, and it had something to do with the jewelry box snuggled safely in her suitcase. Her suitcase! It was still in the car!

At that moment, the back door opened and Augusta strode briskly into the kitchen. Almost immediately upon seeing them, she hesitated. To Kit it seemed as though a second woman emerged. Her aunt shed the guise of a purposeful dynamic career woman and took on one of the indecisive, fearful, aging old maid so familiar to Kit.

"Kit, *Goddag. Hur står det till?*" Augusta hesitated, then switched to English. "I forget you don't speak much Swedish. How are you? You got here all right? And your luggage, did Lars take it into my bedroom as I instructed him? Or maybe—"

"My suitcase is still in the car."

Augusta immediately headed toward the living room and Kit followed, arriving in time to witness her aunt accosting Lars.

"Lars why haven't you brought Kit's bags into the house? Please do so as soon as possible."

Sullenly, Lars stared at the tall woman. "I'll get to it sooner or later."

"Uncle Edmund," Augusta appealed to her uncle. "Will you please tell Lars to retrieve the bags? I'd like to get Kit settled in before dinner. It's not courteous to leave her bags out in the car. "

Edmund glared at his son with a peculiar glitter that made Kit shiver. "You heard her, son."

Tension crackled in the gloomy room between father and son. With a telling glance toward his father, Lars rolled to his feet. "Okay. Okay," he grunted. "Don't get yer dander up. I'll get 'em."

As he lumbered out the door, his worn jeans sagged around his hips and brushed the carpet under the heels of his costly half-laced sneakers.

"If you will, Lars. Thank you. And Kit," said Augusta. "I'll help you get settled."

Augusta led the way to her bedroom, which Kit knew held twin beds. She hadn't forgotten the rose wallpaper, rose-colored bedspreads, or the daintily crocheted rose doilies that decorated the lamp stand and chest of drawers. Most of all, she hadn't forgotten the smell of lilacs that permeated the room; a sharp contrast with its rose theme.

Her aunt's long, tapered fingers smoothed down the spread on the bed closest to the wall near the door. "This one is yours. It will make it a few steps nearer the bathroom. May I help you put your things away?"

Carefully Kit lowered herself onto the bed, swung forward and up. She breathed a sigh of relief; she'd be able to get up from the bed without assistance. Had it been any lower...she didn't want to think about the difficulty she'd have then.

Lars barged in without knocking, lugging her light suitcase. "Here." He dumped it ungraciously onto the bed and stomped out with, "That better be all."

"Thank you, Lars," Augusta called to his retreating form. Kit pursed her lips to keep her thoughts to herself.

"Katalina, let me help you unpack."

Kit stalled. "Why don't I just hand you the things that need to be hung up." She clicked open the case. For some reason she didn't want anyone to question her about the jewelry box, not even her aunt who'd conveyed Gramma Clara's request to her over the phone.

Unfolding a long, navy skirt with matching jacket she handed it, along with a silky white blouse, to her aunt. Augusta scrutinized the ensemble approvingly. "Is this all you have? We do dress for dinner, you remember." Silently Kit handed her a long, elegantly simple royal blue gown whose sleeves and hem-flounce were edged with white lace. She added a burgundy satin blouse. "To go with the skirt," she explained.

Again her aunt questioned, "This is all?"

Surveying her aunt's expensive suit, one Kit knew she herself could never afford, she held back a retort. Somehow, even in her expensive clothes, her aunt always seemed to be just slightly dated. Her faded blue or drab gray skirts, regardless of fashion, were always worn midi-length. Augusta bought plain white blouses with childish peter pan collars. She wore her hair in short, tight curls, and her thin lips never felt the touch of lipstick, nor her pale cheeks, blush. *Poor Aunt Augusta*, thought Kit, her anger evaporating.

"If you'll tell me where," Kit said, smiling, "I'll put the rest away myself."

Augusta glanced nervously at Kit's comfortable slacks and casual top. Kit could never remember seeing her aunt in slacks and, though Kit sensed her aunt's disapproval, Augusta merely turned to pull open a drawer. "You can keep your things here. All right? Is it low enough for you? Maybe it's too heavy."

Her aunt's solicitude grated on Kit. She was hard pressed to still the senseless irritation that reared its head whenever her independence was questioned...even when done with her well being in mind. Dr. Ellis came to mind.

"No, it's just fine, thanks." She hoped her aunt didn't noticed the unintended sharpness of her tone. "I can handle it now, Aunt Augusta."

Swiftly Kit fitted her slacks, tops, and underclothes into the drawer. After a moment's hesitation, she left the jewelry box in her suitcase. Snapping the suitcase shut, she set it on the floor behind the bed.

"If you're sure you can manage...If you don't need anything else..."

"I'm fine, Auntie, really."

"All right then. In that case I best be helping Sally get dinner on. *God afton.* Good evening." Augusta smiled thinly, leaving Kit smiling in amusement after her. She wondered if her aunt sprinkled her speech at work with Swedish, her first language.

Still smiling, Kit shut the drawer and picked up her small Bible where she'd laid it on the nightstand between the beds. She was about to sit down and open it when Sally stuck her head in the doorway. "Dearie, Clara's awake, and she's asking for you."

CHAPTER FIVE

Bread of deceit is sweet to a man; but afterwards his mouth shall be filled with gravel. Proverbs 20:17

After Keith registered for his conference at the tall opulent convention center, he secured a comfortable car and made his way north to Anoka, a suburb of the Minneapolis-St. Paul metropolis. Since their recent move, he hadn't seen his sister Beth, her husband John, or their two children, Heidi Jo and Lisa. Her enthusiastic letters made him anxious to see their new home along the banks of the Mississippi River.

During the drive, his mind turned toward Kit. He could still feel the softness of her skin on his palm, as though branded. Images of her head snuggled against his shoulder brought forth a gentle smile. Their conversations made him shake his head. Kit Anderson had a beauty all her own, a beauty without artifice. He rather liked the way her eyes widened as she gazed up at him.

He'd thought her a child, yet her mind was as agile as any he'd ever known. Obviously well read, as well as intelligent, Kit's take on the issues they talked about made him reconsider at some points. She was sharp, all right.

Ken Ellis had placed her under his protection and she trusted him. Had he let her down by allowing her to go with her cousin? She was out of his life for the time being. Isn't that what he wanted?

No, he admitted to himself with a frown, *no it wasn't.*Not that he had a romantic interest, of course, but he *had* promised. He was a person who kept his promises. A slight smile touched the corners of his lips. He'd call her...soon.

Deep in his thoughts, Keith almost missed the Anoka sign. Turning off the highway, he focused on watching the street signs as they flashed by. Another turn and he slowed to search for the address. There it was. As he beheld the two-story house of dark native wood, it reminded him of a resort cottage he once stayed in. The thought flashed in his mind that Kit might enjoy staying here. He could imagine the light in her eyes if he took her boating on the river. He shook himself mentally. There was little likelihood she'd come here, or have reason too. So why did the thought persist?

While Keith drove to his sister's new home, Kit quietly tiptoed across the hall through the door into Gramma Clara's bedroom. The last rays from the late afternoon sun streamed across the bed, giving it an insubstantial quality. The fragile form on the bed shifted slightly and Kit knew her grandmother was watching her.

Clara held out a parchment-like, work-worn hand. "Kit, you gave me quite a shock just now."

"Gramma?" Kit moved toward the bed.

"Kit, for a second you took me back many, many *året*...years." Clara spoke softly, but with surprising strength. "Anyone ever tell you how much you look like your namesake, Katalina? Your blood grandmother, and my best friend?"

Kit shook her head. "Sally said I reminded her of Mom."

The old woman surveyed her granddaughter, her eyes glistening with a shimmer of tears. "*Ya,* you have Sophia's strength, I think, and her determination. Katalina was not physically strong. Slight she was, and pretty. With a smile that warmed whatever room she entered. Just like yours."

"Strong?" Kit held out her hands and glanced down at her legs. "Gramma, I'm not strong at all. I'm weak."

Clara grasped Kit's hand. "Not physical strength, Kit, inner strength. Only inner strength could have kept you going through all that you have. You are strong...stronger, I fear, than I...." Her words trailed off.

Kit stared at her grandmother. "I...I don't understand."

"You will, Katalina. You will." Her eyes clouding for a moment as though she looked into the distant past, Clara sighed. Her attention snapped back. "*Var så god och sitt ner.*"

Kit's legs had begun to ache from standing so still. As though noticing her grimace of pain, Gramma Clara released Kit's hands. "Sit down, Kit. *Ya*, you need to sit down. You are tired."

Kit nodded. "It's been a long day."

At her grandmother's request she thankfully pulled up the vanity bench and sat down. Smiling, Clara patted her hand, drinking in the girl's presence as though gathering strength from her.

"You have questions, *ya*?"

"Gramma, I don't understand why you wanted me to bring the jewelry box. Did you want it back?"

"*Ach*, no, Kit. It is yours, and rightfully so. I just needed to see it, to touch it, and to hold it once more before I die." As usual the old woman minced no words.

"I think I understand," Kit said slowly. "When Mom died, I held that box. It was somehow comforting to know it was part of my heritage...I still had roots, but...."

"But you cannot see what this has to do with me. Didn't you know the box was once mine?"

Kit's eyes widened. "No!"

Clara smiled, a soft faraway smile. "I thought not. Let me tell you." She closed her eyes. Kit felt her drifting back to a time long past. When Clara again opened her eyes they focused on the far wall. "I remember Katalina so well...small, pretty, always smiling. *Ya*, Katalina was my very best friend in all the world. We did everything together. Orphaned at seven, she was taken in and brought up by her uncle and godfather."

"Wasn't he the famous Swedish songwriter, A. L. Augustafson?"

"*Ya*, Sophia told you. That is good." Clara paused as though collecting strength to continue. "Already old when he took in his niece, it wasn't many years before Augustafson needed her to take care of him. She didn't mind. He had been very good to her, and Katalina loved him as a father."

"The problem was that Edmund was already in love with her and her constant care of her uncle angered him," Clara sighed.

"He demanded she spend more and more time with him. 'Uncle needs me,' she told him, but he wasn't satisfied with the time she allowed herself away from her beloved uncle.

"Finally, Edmund took matters into his own hands. When Augustafson lost his hired hand, Edmund took the job to help with the heavier tasks about the farm. He took the job to be near Kat since he stayed right on the property in a room over the barn." Clara smiled sadly. "I thought then my best friend would one day be my sister-in-law. Back then Edmund was tall, blond, and very debonair. His pride and joy was his long, bushy mustache. *Ya*, back then he was a handsome lad."

Kit, listening in fascination to the story, heard a painful sadness creep into the old woman's voice. Clara stopped for so long, Kit wondered if she was still awake.

"Gramma?" she asked softly. "Gramma?"

With a start Clara continued. "Then...Katalina's uncle died. He burned to death when the candles on the Christmas tree caught fire." She focused sad eyes on Kit. "*Ya*, in the old days before electricity, we put candles on the tree for light. Katalina and Ed were thankful to get out alive. Later she found the jewelry box perfectly intact among the ruins of the house.

"She lost her parents at such a young age, and then this. It was all too much for poor Katalina. She ran away, away from the past, away from Ed, away to America to begin a new life."

Intrigued, Kit leaned forward as Clara's voice faded to a whisper.

"In Clayton Wisconsin she met strong, capable Claus. Though he was older by ten years, he loved gentle Katalina in a way Ed could never understand. He was a good man, was Claus, and Katalina married him. *Ya*, she wrote me of her happiness. I still remember that letter from my dear friend. So full of love, she was, love and hope for the future. I was so happy for her, but Edmund was not. I knew then Edmund was just too immature, too full of boyish pranks for someone like Katalina, who needed someone she could depend on." Pausing, Clara sighed deeply before continuing.

"I missed her, but wished her well." Clara clutched Kit's hand, her voice low. "Later word came that my dearest friend died giving birth to your mother."

Kit gulped. She'd never heard this story. All she could get out of her mother was that Kit's real grandmother died when she was very young. Her mother seldom spoke of the past. She answered Kit's persistent questions; first with reluctance, and then irritation. Her evasiveness only fueled Kit's curiosity about the past. At last she knew the truth.

Clara continued softly, tiredly. "Claus deeply grieved his young wife. In his pain and loneliness he rented out his farm, packed up and brought little Sophia to Sweden. He came to find that Katalina's friends, as well as his own family, had either died or also immigrated to America. By then Edmund, grieving in his own way, had joined the army and was far away. In trying to ease each other's grief, Claus and I fell in love." A tender smile played about her lips. "Soon we married and I became Sophia's mother. A couple years went by and we had Augusta.

"I was very happy, but Claus was restless for his farm in America. Once again he packed up, this time to return with his new family to America. I left my home in Sweden never to return. It didn't matter. I had Claus."

"The jewelry box, Gramma," Kit asked quietly, "what about the jewelry box?"

"*Ya*, the box. Claus gave it to me, Katalina's box, for a wedding gift. He told me 'Clara, have this. It is Katalina's love and Katalina's blessing I want us to have. Only it must go to Sophia when she grows up.' So the box was mine, for a time. When your mother married and went away with that handsome preacher of hers, I passed it on to her as Claus requested. It was hers by right."

Again Clara was silent, her hand gripping Kit's, surprisingly strong. "How was I to know when I came to America, that Ed, too, would come? How was I to know that my dear Claus would die, leaving me alone with the farm and two young girls to raise? Then Sophia...." Sighing, Clara slumped against the pillows, her voice hollow. "It is past my time. I am ready to go. I want to see Katalina and Claus and Sophia again."

"Gramma, do you want me to bring you the jewelry box?"

Opening her eyes, Clara traced Kit's gnarled fingers. "*Ya*, I want to see the box once more, but I have no wish to bring my troubles upon you. You've been through so much..."

Kit stared at her grandmother in confusion. "Trouble. What trouble?"

Abruptly Clara changed the subject. "Are you happy?"

"Yes, Gramma."

"Have you anyone to look out for you?"

Remembering all too well Keith's intense gaze and the warmth of his embrace, Kit hoped Gramma Clara wouldn't notice her clenched hands or the sudden jump in her heart rate. Clearing her throat, she said, "If you mean, did I come to Minneapolis alone, no. Dr. Long, an associate of my orthopedist, traveled with me. He has a conference in town this week."

"And this man, he is special to you?" Gramma's intense questioning brought a blush to Kit's pale cheeks. Her grandmother noticed far too much!

Hastily Kit answered, "Oh, no, Gramma. Dr. Long is a very kind man, but I only just met him before we flew to Minneapolis. My doctor, Dr. Ellis, asked him to watch out for me since he didn't think I should travel alone."

"He is a good man, your doctor." It was a statement.

"Yes, Gramma."

"And this Dr. Long, you like him, *ya*?"

Kit glanced away, but her stained cheeks surely gave her away. What harm could there be in telling her grandmother the truth? "I do like him, Gramma, but it's different for him. He'd never look at someone like me."

"And vy not? You're a lovely young woman, Kit. He'll see that, if he's the right one. Remember that." The old woman lay back against her pillows exhausted. "Kit...."

At that moment, Sally looked in on them. Efficiently, she checked Clara's pulse.

"Kit, I think you'd better leave. I'm afraid Clara has overextended herself."

Nodding, Kit moved to get up, but Clara gripped her hand. "Wait! Kit will leave in a moment, Sally. Give us a moment."

"A minute then." Frowning, Sally left the room, only to pop back in. "I'll be back, so make it quick."

As the door closed, Clara leaned forward. "The jewelry box, Katalina. Have you told anyone about the jewelry box?"

"No, why? Shall I bring it now?"

Clara pursed her lips. Shaking her head she mumbled, "No time now. Promise you won't let anyone know about it...promise!"

"Of course I promise. But Aunt Augusta knows. On the phone she asked me to bring it."

"I'm not concerned with her knowing this. Just, just..."

"I won't show it to anyone, or mention it, Gramma."

Clara's face relaxed. Her grip slackened. A moment later her breathing slowed in sleep. As Kit rose to her feet, she heard Sally's solid practical shoes echoing quietly on the hardwood floor.

Sally put a finger to her lips as Kit tiptoed from the room. Turning toward the living room, Kit hesitated, then went instead to her room. Her talk with her grandmother had taken the last of her resources. Taking off her blouse and slacks, Kit belted on a white terry cloth robe and lay down for a short nap.

Sometime later, feeling much more refreshed, she headed toward the bathroom where she quickly washed up before returning to the bedroom. Taking out her long royal blue gown, Kit slipped it on, and relished the silky smoothness against her skin. After snapping a shiny, wide black belt around her waist, Kit clasped a gold necklace around her neck to match the bracelet on her wrist. With a comb tacked at a convenient angle onto a two-foot polished handle so she could reach her hair with it, she combed out her long hair, leaving it hanging down her back in natural waves.

Critically, Kit stared at herself in the mirror. Deciding she could do no better, she reluctantly limped out into the living room. There Lars still lounged on the sofa, idly flipping through a magazine. Edmund hunched in Clara's favorite overstuffed chair in the corner. In his hand he held an hourglass that he turned over and over as the sand trickled through the narrow opening. Carefully he set the glass on the lamp table nearby, only to pick it up again.

The lamplight cast shadows over Edmund's sunken face, giving him a half-angelic, half-demonic appearance. Outside, the wind whipped through the juniper bushes drawing eerie shadows across the curtains.

Shuddering, Kit decided she preferred reading a book in her room while awaiting dinner. Unfortunately she hesitated too long.

From the recesses of his chair her great uncle whined, "Katalina, come here."

Compassion for the old man filled Kit and she stepped on into the living room. *Poor man. Must be lonely sitting around day after day with nothing better to do than to wait for his sister to die.*

The word "dismal" snapped into her thoughts, yet never before had she considered Gramma Clara's home dismal. The rich yellow of the large rug in the center of the room and the cheerful print on the sofa and chairs were anything but dismal. Seven years ago this was a home, a room filled with contentment, with laughter, with peace.

Had seven years changed all that, or had Gramma's illness? *No,* Kit decided, pulling over the piano bench and sitting down next to the old man. It was not the room, but the occupants of the room, a pathetic old man and an even more pathetic son and the constantly drawn curtains, that made the difference.

"Uncle Edmund, how are you?"

"I am not so fine these days, Katalina. Why do you come? Why come now?"

"Gramma Clara asked for me."

Edmund's eyebrows rose. "Messing into things again, is she?" His voice grated with surprising harshness.

"What are you talking about Uncle Edmund?"

The old man shook his head. "Nothing. Nothing. Why did you come?" he whined.

"Because Gramma Clara asked for me," Kit answered again, wishing mightily she'd stayed in her room.

"She doesn't need you. She has Augusta. She has me. She has...Lars."

Kit bit back the sarcastic comment about Lars that came to mind. Instead she said, "Gramma probably really wants Mom, but...I'm all she has left."

"Sophia would have seen to things properly. Always capable that one, always determined, but too stubborn. What good are you?"

Lars entered the conversation. "You might as well go home. You're just excess baggage around here anyway. Sally does what needs doing. Who needs you?"

Kit flushed angrily. To her astonishment, Edmund jumped to her defense. "Don't mind the boy, Katalina. He never did know how to behave himself around a pretty girl." He gazed at her so intently Kit's angry flush turned to one of shy embarrassment.

Deliberately staring at her hands, Lars mocked, "Pretty? You? I don't think so. I thought the old man's mind was on the blink. Now I *know* it."

Kit closed her eyes. Pain twisted deep inside her. Crossing her arms, she tucked the offending appendages from sight. The room grew cold and unfriendly. In confusion, she jerked to her feet.

"Maybe Aunt Augusta could use some help in the kitchen," she mumbled over her shoulder as she hurried from the room.

The warm aroma of hot, tender roast, hot, fresh blueberry muffins, piping hot potatoes and beans, and the sight of the friendly comradeship between Augusta and Sally as they worked side by side preparing the meal eased some of Kit's tension. She wanted to feel needed, or was it the other way around? "May I help? Please?"

Sally chuckled. "Dearie, as you can see, this kitchen is a tight fit even for the two of us who are used to working together. Besides, we have dinner well in hand. You go relax."

"Why not talk to Uncle Edmund for a while?" Augusta suggested.

"I...tried that." No way would she go back. And the kitchen was obvious off limits, which she could well understand. If Augusta had not been so thin she never would have been able to move around Sally's bulk.

At home, in her apartment, dishes, pans, and silverware were all within reach. But here...Disappointment curled inside. "Maybe I could set the table."

Her aunt smiled. "Now that's a good idea, Kit. Sally, should I get the dishes for Kit, or will you?"

"I'm closer. Here dearie." The stout woman handed Kit a stack of china dinner plates. She piled heavy silverware on top, until Kit feared she'd drop the whole stack.

"Thanks," she managed to say before staggering into the dining room.

Carefully Kit avoided one of the many throw rugs, most made by Gramma Clara, that her aunt liked to have scattered throughout the house. She envisioned catching her toe, falling, and sending the fine china dishes crashing about her in all directions. Thankfully it was not but a few steps from the kitchen to the oak dining table.

Sally had already added another leaf to the table and covered it with one of the snowy-white linen tablecloths Gramma Clara had woven in Sweden before she came to America. Kit sidled past the tall cabinet whose glass door showed off the priceless Sevrés china and Dresden figurines on its shelves. The sideboard under the window held some of the many plants Gramma loved and tended so carefully before her illness, as well as two silver tea sets, one on either end.

A small end table by the hallway held a phone and the thick city directory. Kit managed to edge about the crowded room setting the table, and adding the crystal goblets from the cabinet. She was thankful Sally hadn't added any more leaves or there wouldn't have been room to slide between the furniture and the table.

Moments after Kit set down the last goblet, Augusta stuck her head into the dining room. "Dinner," she called. Kit congratulated herself on her timing. Smiling in satisfaction she stood at the table, and waited while the others assembled.

While Sally and her aunt brought the steaming plates and bowls to the table, along with several salads and homemade jam, Uncle Edmund shuffled past her into the hallway. When he returned, he wore a tie and had tidied his thin, straggly white hair.

Lars came to the table as he was, and only went to wash up at Augusta's rebuke and Sally's glare. Returning after the others already found their places, he balked at sitting next to Kit. "I'm not sitting next to her."

"Lars!" her aunt gasped, nonplused.

Kit bit her lip. She wouldn't cry. She wouldn't!

Calmly, Sally propelled herself to her feet. "Sit here then. I'll sit next to Kit."

She settled back down, this time beside Kit as Lars took Sally's place across the table. "Uncle Edmund," Augusta requested in her quiet tone, "please say grace."

Kit caught the sneer on Lars' face as she closed her eyes. She expected to hear some nasty crack, but he kept still. Hurriedly Uncle Edmund mumbled some words Kit couldn't understand. She did catch the loud, "amen." After praying her own prayer, Kit glanced up to find everyone waiting for her.

Soon platters of delicious smelling food were passed around the table. Kit did full justice to the meal. After the first pangs had been satisfied, conversation picked up. Augusta began, "Uncle, what did you find to do today?"

Lars jeered. "What he usually does, slump in that stupid chair and rot."

Sally glared at the insolent Lars. "And of what use were you around the house today?"

"Well, I did go pick up my little crip of a gold diggin' cousin."

It was Kit's turn to glare at him. Instead she smiled, catching her cousin completely by surprise. Sally stifled a chuckle. "I'd suggest being nice to your cousin, Lars, but it probably wouldn't do any good."

They exchanged a long speculative look. Tension stretched between them. Kit hurried to change the subject.

"Did you know I was named for my grandmother, my real grandmother Katalina? Gramma was telling me all about her this afternoon."

Four forks jerked to a halt halfway to four mouths. Sally recovered first, but her hearty smile appeared forced. "What did Clara tell you about her, dearie?"

Kit glanced at her great uncle. "She told me you used to court Katalina, Uncle Edmund."

Edmund nodded, his thin lips tight. No one spoke.

"What happened?" prodded Kit to fill the uncomfortable silence. "Poor Katalina running away to America. Why didn't you go with her Uncle Edmund?"

Rolling his eyes, Lars prompted contemptuously. "Well, father?"

"We were young. She ran out on...." Edmund's pale cheeks reddened in anger. "She never would listen to me."

"But if you loved her couldn't you have followed her?"

Edmund glared at her. "What good would that have done? By then she was already married to the old dirt farmer."

Augusta flushed, and her fingers played nervously with her fork. "Uncle," she said quietly, "my father was a prosperous and well respected farmer."

Lars shrugged. "Kat ran out because of the big fire, didn't she?"

Edmund turned, if possible, even redder. His fist crashed down on the table with unexpected force. "Shut up!" He went on to speak some harsh words that, though spoken in his native tongue, Kit had no trouble understanding.

In the ensuing silence, Edmund picked up his fork. His hand shook so much he dropped it again. Kit finished eating in silence, her head bowed. This was her fault. She wished she could drop through the floor out of sight. Why had she opened her mouth?

Still, glancing up at her great uncle, Kit was puzzled. There were still missing pieces. Somehow, she couldn't yet put it together.

With a sigh, she wished for Keith's calm, logical mind and sound advice. He'd know what to make of the strange situation in which she found herself. Closing her eyes, she prayed for wisdom.

CHAPTER SIX

"...I have dreamed a dream, and my spirit was troubled to know the dream." Daniel 2:3

In the vortex of hostility crackling around the table, Kit felt small and vulnerable. If only she hadn't delved into the past, and yet...even yet she wanted to learn more. She yearned for answers with a desire that surprised her. Why all the secrecy? Why the hostility...the fear?

Kit tried to break through the swirling tension. "Uncle Edmund, when did you first come to America?"

Edmund frowned as everyone looked toward him silently, expectantly. "Forty...four, no," he hastened to correct himself, "forty-three years ago. I immigrated the year after Claus died." He glanced surreptitiously at Augusta whose hands nervously fingered the stem of her glass.

Edmund straightened his thin shoulders. "Yes, that was when I came over. You do remember don't you Augusta? No, maybe again you wouldn't."

Lars grunted. "I guess you wouldn't at that." He rolled his eyes.

Puzzled Kit spoke up, "Why not? How old were you when Uncle Edmund immigrated, Aunt Augusta?"

Augusta concentrated on her ice cream. "Fifteen." she said quietly.

"Fifteen. And you don't remember?"

Regarding Kit through unsympathetic eyes, Sally patted her hand as though to quiet her. "Dearie, at the time, your aunt was in the hospital."

Kit choked on her spoonful of ice cream. "I didn't know," she said. "I'm sorry."

Lars mocked, "One of the family's skeletons right, Augusta?"

With quiet dignity, Augusta said, "Sally, there's no need to protect me. Kit is family. She has a right to know." Taking a deep breath, Augusta stared down at her bowl. "Kit, I was in a sanitarium. You see, after Dad di...passed away, I had a nervous breakdown." She tried to smile, but failed. Carefully setting her spoon on her plate, she picked nervously at the napkin in her lap.

"After I got out neither Sophia nor Mama would let anyone talk about it because...because it bothered me so much."

"Kit," explained Sally, her lips crinkling into a smile. "Augusta doesn't remember much of anything that went on that year or so after her father's death."

"Because she was in the loony bin," added Lars.

"Sanitarium," corrected Sally firmly. "She has no recollection of what happened the night her father died." At the word "died," Augusta clenched her fist as though in pain.

"Doesn't matter now," Edmund said. "That's all ancient history, if you ask me. Katalina, let Augusta alone. Some things are better off forgotten."

His eyes focused on Augusta with a deep sadness Kit took as compassion. Far from being a senile old man, Edmund now seemed quite in control of his faculties, his mind sharp.

But, thought Kit, not sharp enough.

Can't he see, can't they all see that forgetting the past hasn't worked for Augusta? All the secrecy seems to have done is force her to hide away the fears and pain of that long ago night. Maybe Aunt Augusta would be better off if her fears were brought out in the open. Maybe then they'd lose their hold. Not only over her, but over everyone else as well.

She opened her mouth to speak but her aunt interrupted nervously, "The roast was wonderful, Sally. Thank you."

"Great cookin' as always Sally." Leaning back, Lars patted his paunch. "I'm stuffed."

Augusta protested as Lars pulled out a cigar and lit up. "Lars, please. Think of mother. Smoke isn't good for her lungs and you know it."

"Augusta's right, Lars." Sally scowled at his sneer. "The smoke may be harmful to Clara."

Lars' eyes narrowed as he stared at the nurse. "Don't worry, she's safely tucked away in her bedroom. Besides, the quicker she goes the better."

Augusta gasped. "Lars!" She appealed to her uncle. "Uncle Edmund, please."

With a dismissive shrug, Edmund staggered to his feet. Once again he seemed lost in some world of his own. Kit saw Lars' lips twist contemptuously as his father hobbled back to his place in the living room. Disgusted, Kit swung to her feet, leaving Lars to smoke his pungent cigar alone. At the door of the kitchen, Kit glanced back when she heard the chair creak. Lars lurched to his feet and sauntered into the living room, a fog of smoke trailing behind him.

In the kitchen she found Augusta crying into the dishwater. "Aunt Augusta, what's wrong?"

Wiping her hands on a dishtowel, her aunt took a delicately embroidered handkerchief from her apron pocket and blew her nose. "I'm all right," she said. "Really I am."

"If you're sure." Kit hesitated.

"Why don't you clear the table, Kit? If you don't mind, that is?"

"I don't mind, Auntie." Awkwardly patting her aunt's arm, Kit returned to the dining room to clear the table. Thankfully, though the smell from the cigar lingered, the smoke had dissipated.

She found Sally busily stacking the dishes and setting the pile of plates on the counter along with the silverware. As Kit cleared the goblets, Sally went to check on Clara. When she didn't return, Kit went to help her aunt with the dishes.

Taking the towel her aunt handed her, Kit said, "Lars is awfully rude."

"I know," Augusta said. Pulling out the now crumpled handkerchief, Augusta wiped her nose. "I never could get along with him. Not even when we were children, though he was much younger than I. He was either lazy, mischievous, or violent."

"Do you have to put up with him staying here all the time?"

Her aunt's shoulders slumped. "For now, I suppose. Maybe, after Mother passes on and the estate is finally settled...I don't know...he is my cousin."

Kit wiped the heavy platter, almost dropping it in the process. "Not a very nice one," she muttered, relieved to set the platter on the counter.

Augusta heard. "I know. I'm sorry about how he treats you, Kit, how he treats everyone. So much is happening right now. I know mother asked for you, but maybe I shouldn't have asked you to come. Maybe—"

Kit bit her lip, sensing her aunt was about to break into tears again. They finished the dishes in silence. As her aunt put the dried dishes back in the cupboards, Kit returned to the bedroom to read the mystery book she'd brought along. She thought she'd have time to read on the trip to the city, but found her conversation with Dr. Long much more interesting. Even thinking about him made her pulse jump.

By now he was busy with his conference and had probably forgotten all about her. *It doesn't matter,* she told herself. Isn't that what she expected? They'd been traveling companions, nothing more. *All right, all right, so he's more than that to me,* Kit admitted to herself. *That isn't going to change how he feels about me. What if...?* She refused to let such an impossible fantasy continue. No, no way. She stared at her hands. How could he ever...? How could any man accept her just as she was?

Shaking her head, Kit forced herself to think of something, anything else. What was the matter with her? She'd come into the bedroom to read her book. Now where had she put it? *That's right,* she thought, *I left it in the case along with the jewelry box.*

Lugging out her suitcase, she swung it onto the bed and unsnapped the locks. Opening it, her heartbeat stopped. Yes, there was the book all right, but the jewelry box was gone!

Who'd taken it? Who other than her grandmother and her aunt even knew she had it? Could her aunt have placed it somewhere else? Kit checked around the room to no avail. Where was it? Why would someone take it? It had sentimental value, true. It was probably an antique, but her grandmother had lots of antiques—most of them in plain sight. Why take this one? Kit's head pounded.

If only she could run to her grandmother, but she mustn't worry her. She considered talking to Augusta? No, she'd promised her grandmother she wouldn't speak of the box to anyone. Besides, Aunt Augusta had quite enough on her mind as it was.

Restlessly, Kit sat down and opened her book. Over and over she read the same pages without understanding more than a word or two. As the room grew dark she switched on the lamp between the beds. She thought of Edmund turning over the hourglass. Wasn't she doing something similar by simply marking time? Slamming the book closed, she set it on the nightstand beside her well-worn Bible and lay back on the bed.

Round and round the situation played in her mind as she stared at the ceiling. If the house wasn't so full of people, she might try searching for the jewelry box. Maybe she'd look around after her aunt went to bed. She shook her head. Yes, she could try, but if it wasn't in plain sight it was unlikely she'd find it. She couldn't get up on a ladder or down on the floor to search.

Sighing, Kit unbuckled her belt. She might as well retire for the night. Things might look more hopeful tomorrow. A sharp knock at the door startled her. "Hey," called Lars, "phone for ya."

She hadn't even heard it ring. Who would be calling for her now? Dr. Ellis maybe? Surely it wouldn't be...Keith? A gladness welled up in her until her hands trembled as she quickly rebuckled her belt. True, he'd promised to call, but she hadn't really expected him to keep that promise. Nonetheless, her heart raced as she picked up the receiver. "Hello."

"Kit, Keith Long here."

Gladness washed over her in such waves she reached for the nearby chair. "Spock, I mean, K— Dr. Long." Somehow with the many listening ears she just could *not* address the man informally. "I'm so glad to hear from you."

Keith wondered if the anxious undertone he heard was real or a product of his own concern. "Are you all right?"

This time he didn't mistake her hesitation. "I arrived safely," she said.

"How is your grandmother?" Keith sensed something amiss and wished he'd followed his first instinct to drive over to see her. He pictured her oval face, the wide eyes, those kissable lips.

He almost missed her strained, "Everyone believes it's but a matter of time."

Keith frowned, wondering who "everyone" referred to. "Kit, are you all right?" he asked again.

Again the long pause and the careful words, "It's not what I expected."

"Can you tell me about it?" He found himself gripping the phone.

"Not really, not now." He heard her deep sigh.

"I take it there are others within listening distance."

"That's it, Sp— Dr. Long. But, really, I am doing as well as can be expected under the circumstances."

"Um, are you trying to convince me or yourself?"

Kit spoke hastily as though she feared Keith might become bored with her long silences and stumbling manner. She probably thought he was only doing his duty in checking up on her.

He winced. Had he been so transparent?

"Dr. Long, how is your sister and family?" She sounded breathless.

"They're fine, Kit. I wish you could meet them. I know you and Beth would like each other." Sensing her insecurity, Keith went on to detail the house and his reception. He had her giggling at the ankle biting he'd received from their furry black and white mongrel puppy, Cutie.

"That's my special friend," he said softly. "Feeling better now?"

"Yes, yes I am." He heard a quick intake of breath as though that surprised her.

"Is there some way you can explain what's bothering you?"

Again she hesitated. "I don't think so."

"Someone always there?"

"Afraid so. Always."

He knew she was trying to explain why she couldn't talk freely. He told himself it was none of his affair. Hadn't he done more than he agreed to by checking up on her? Still, her large, innocent eyes haunted him. He knew she desperately wanted to talk to him. Hadn't he agreed to watch out for her? Wasn't this, too, part of his Christian duty? He sighed.

If he was honest with himself, he knew he wanted to see her again. Was she really as lovely as he remembered? Lovely? Pleasant looking maybe, but lovely? A grin tugged his lips. Yes, lovely. Or were his standards changing?

"Look, Kit. Do you have plans for tomorrow, say about noon?" His grin widened.

"No, I don't think so. Why?"

"I'd like you to come out to the house to meet my sister Beth. We'll *do* lunch." Keith drawled his invitation with a decided British accent. Kit's giggle rewarded him.

"Quite so, m'lord. I am honored you should stoop to favor a poor maiden such as I."

"Of course, my dear. You will come?"

"This for real?" Her genuine surprise brought an unexpected laugh to his lips. His deep laugh made his sister, sitting nearby watching a movie, glance at him in surprise. "Is it all right with your sister?"

"Sure, but if it will ease your mind, I'll ask." Turning from the phone, he asked loudly enough for Kit to hear, "Beth, it's all right if I bring a guest for dinner tomorrow, isn't it?"

"Why of course, Keith, but what about your conference?"

Kit echoed the question on the phone. "I don't want you to miss your conference on my account."

Her sincerity was unmistakable. He smiled as he spoke to her. "Don't you worry. I won't miss but a boring session or two. I'll pick you up about eleven, all right?"

Hanging up the phone, he met his sister's inquiring gaze. "Who's this woman you want to impress?"

Keith frowned. "I'm not trying to impress anyone. Just thought I'd get Kit away for a while. Didn't sound like things were too pleasant at her grandmother's place. I thought she might enjoy a picnic out on the terrace."

"Kit? Oh, the young disabled woman you escorted to Minneapolis."

"Yes." Picking up a folder, he stood up and effectively ended the conversation. "I think I'll go on up to my room."

He didn't need to see Beth to know she watched him with a musing light in her gold-flecked blue eyes.

For a moment longer, Kit held the phone as though to prolong contact with Keith. The sound of his deep voice echoed in her mind, surrounding her with a sense of security and warmth. Independence, as nice as it might be, didn't seem near so attractive as a tall, handsome psychologist's arms.

Slowly hanging up the receiver, Kit headed toward the bedroom only to be interrupted by Edmund's jealous whine. "Another beau, Katalina?"

Kit swung about so quickly she almost lost her balance. "What did you say, Uncle Edmund?"

"He thinks you're Katalina, his lost love." Lars rolled his eyes in disgust.

Kit glanced quickly at her uncle, who seemed to shriveled into himself at his son's attack. "No, Uncle Edmund," she said quietly. "It was a friend, simply a friend. Good night." Her security faded like morning fog.

As she hurried back to the bedroom, she felt Lars' gaze like a dagger stabbing into her back. *Where are Aunt Augusta and Sally? Were they with Gramma Clara, or in the kitchen?* She thought better of braving Lars and his father again, and stayed in the bedroom. Something akin to panic stirred inside her and she chided herself for acting as hysterical as the heroine in her mystery novel.

Quickly, Kit slipped out of her gown and pulled a long, thin lace nightgown over her head. Belting on her short robe, she took care of her personal needs in the bathroom before returning to the bedroom. Sitting on the bed, she picked up her Bible. The events of the day exhausted her not only physically, but mentally and spiritually as well.

Flipping open the well-worn holy book, Kit turned to Ephesians 6 and prayed for words not only of comfort, but also of strength. Glancing at the chapter she read, "Finally, my brethren, be strong in the Lord, and in the power of his might." She read the chapter to its end, then read it again more slowly, savoring it like a satisfying meal.

Anxiety and confusion faded from her mind, and the comfort and strength she desired filled her. In the strange situation she found herself in, there was so little she could do on her own. But God promised her strength. He promised all the strength she needed.

Lord, why am I here? Even though Gramma enjoys my company, I can't see that my presence is really necessary. Instead, I feel I'm causing problems for Aunt Augusta, maybe Gramma as well. She paused. *As for Keith....* she couldn't articulate her hopes and fears.

Discouragement flooded over her again, and she shivered. She sensed such fear in them all, her aunt, her uncle, even in her grandmother who had always seemed so calm and sure of herself...much like Kit's own mother.

"God, why me? Why did you take Mama away? I need her. Gramma needs her. What can I do?" Inside she felt the stirrings of rebellion, and had the sinking feeling that she was as repulsive to her Heavenly Father as she was to her cousin. She had failed before. "Help me, Lord. Please help me. I don't know where to turn."

Even as the cry tore from her confused heart, the image of Dr. Keith Long poured into her mind like warm sunshine. Against her closed lids, she conjured up his huge form, his long arms that had held her so securely, the enigmatic face, his comforting, calm, logical voice.

He seemed closer to her than any of her relatives here. Even the image of his presence calmed her confusion and gave her a sense of security. A smile tugged the corners of her mouth. Tomorrow she'd see him again. Tomorrow she'd ask his advice. He'd know what to do. Somehow she had the feeling Keith would always know just what to do.

Not bothering to ask why thoughts of him brought her such comfort, Kit breathed a simple *Thank you, God*, and slipped under the light cover. A few moments later she fell asleep, a soft smile in her heart and on her lips.

Augusta moved quietly around the room, trying not to wake Kit as she readied herself for bed. She wondered what put the smile on her niece's lips and envied her deep, peaceful slumber. She couldn't recall when her own sleep had been so unencumbered. For years she avoided sleep like an enemy, but it always managed to overcome her. She'd found only one way to banish her fears.

Reaching into the drawer of the nightstand, Augusta pulled out a bottle and snapped off the lid. For a long moment she stared at the small oval pill. For too long it had been her only hope.

Kit fought her own battles with physical pain. She bore the loss of her parents with such fortitude it shamed Augusta. If only she could be as strong as her niece; but she wasn't. Firmly putting the pill in her mouth, Augusta washed it down with the glass of water she'd brought from the bathroom. Then she got in bed and, with a long sigh, closed her eyes.

Kit jerked awake. Flinging back the covers, she sat up. Her eyes strained in the darkness. Silence. What awakened her? A scream. Yes, she'd heard a scream. Had it been merely a dream? She didn't think so, but—

Under her covers, her aunt shifted restlessly. "I did it. I did it. I did it," she moaned. In the light of a thin beam of moonlight, Kit watched her aunt with concern.

Reaching over, Kit gently shook her aunt's shoulder. "Aunt Augusta, are you all right? I think you screamed. Were you having a nightmare?"

Sitting up, the gaunt woman rubbed her face. "Screamed? Did I? I'm sorry to wake you. Don't be concerned, Kit. It...it was just...a dream."

"Nightmare, you mean."

"*Ach, ya*, a nightmare. Mother! I hope I didn't wake mother." Nervously she scrambled out from the covers, then paused. "Do you think I should check on her? But if she is not awake...Oh, I don't know."

"Shh." Kit listened intently. "I think it's all right. I don't hear anything. She must have slept through it."

Augusta lay back down. "If you're sure? I...I don't think I can sleep any more right now."

"I'm wide awake, too. Maybe it would help if you told me about it," offered Kit.

"*Ya*, maybe. So bright, it was," Augusta said softly. For a long moment she hesitated. "I was young and happy. Under a tall, sturdy oak tree I was playing with my favorite dolls in the little dollhouse Papa made for me. Suddenly the tree fell, smashing my house into tiny pieces. Then Papa was lying on the ground next to this long, cold, slimy, yellow yarn-like thing. It was like my doll's hair only it wasn't. As I tried to make sense of it, I felt myself falling into pieces like the dollhouse. That must have been when I screamed."

Kit stared at her through the shadows. "Sounds pretty awful. Have you any idea what caused the nightmare? Was it something I said at the supper table? I seemed to upset everyone."

"I can't say, Kit. I do recall my nightmare had to do with

papa's...passing." She was quiet a long moment. When she spoke, her voice shook. "I...I'm afraid they're coming back."

"What are? What's coming back, Aunt Augusta?"

"The nightmares." Kit saw a shudder shake her aunt's thin body.

"You've had nightmares like this before?"

"*Ya*, after...after...."

"After your father died," Kit finished quietly.

"*Ach, ya*. But it has been a long time now. They were bad at first. Very bad, but they went away. The people at that place, they helped me."

"So you haven't had those nightmares since then?" Kit asked in surprise. "Until tonight."

"None so nightmarish. I...I don't sleep well. I haven't for a long, long time, so I take something to help me." Her aunt shook her head. "Oh dear, I don't know what to do! I don't want them to send me away again!" Kit heard her aunt's very real terror.

"It's only one nightmare, Aunt Augusta. It does *not* mean you're having another break down. Probably the things we talked about at dinner brought it on. Or maybe it's the stress of Gramma's illness."

"Are you sure?" It felt odd to have her aging aunt hold with such desperation to her calming words.

"Yes, I think it's possible."

Augusta gave a deep sigh. Sitting up, she swung her legs to the floor. "You're probably right, Kit. I'm going to check on mother, just to be sure she's all right."

She pulled on a long brocade robe. "Afterwards, I'm going to fix myself some hot milk. Would you like to join me?"

Kit hesitated. Her aunt's lips twitched nervously. "You don't like hot milk, I suppose? You needn't have it hot. Or I can get you some tea. Whatever you prefer."

Kit smiled. "Sure, I'll join you in the kitchen."

The hot milk did calm her aunt. Kit drank hers cold, forcing back one yawn after another until her aunt led the way back to the bedroom. The next moment, it seemed, she awoke to the smell of bacon and eggs. With a groan she slid out of the covers, grabbed her robe and headed to the bathroom.

After a quick shower, she dressed in white slacks with a white silk blouse she left open at the neck. Her damp hair was pulled back from her face with a black headband. After adding a touch of soft rose blush to her pale cheeks, she stared into the mirror frowning. Her face remained far too pale. Picking up a tube, Kit touched the rose lipstick to her lips, and smiled at the result.

In the dining room, her aunt sat finishing up a cup of coffee. "Good morning, Kit."

Kit yawned. "Good morning, Aunt Augusta."

She sat down beside her aunt as Sally brought her a plate of bacon and eggs.

Edmund, sitting across the table, eyed her yawn. "Couldn't sleep, huh."

Kit blinked. "I went to bed early enough and slept until Aunt Augusta woke me up." She spoke without thinking, but even as the words left her mouth she knew she'd made a mistake.

Lars sauntered up to the table, looking slovenly in baggy tan slacks and a wrinkled black and white striped T-shirt. "So cousin woke you up?"

Stifling another yawn, Kit shrugged. "She just had a bad dream."

Edmund glanced sharply at Augusta. "Like the other nightmares?"

Augusta frowned. "I...I suppose it was." She threw Kit a look of desperation. "Kit said it was just due to the talk last night. Please, forget it all of you. I...I'm fine." With a trembling hand, Augusta picked up her cup.

Lars' lips twisted in his customary sneer. "Wouldn't want a repeat performance now, would we...dear cousin?"

Augusta's face lost all color. Her hand gripped her cup with such intensity, Kit wondered why it didn't shatter in her hands. At that moment, Sally bustled in again. This time with a large glass of milk for Kit. "Good morning, Kit. Good morning, Lars. Sit down. I'll get you a plate."

Lars took his plate without a thank you, and wolfed down his breakfast like he hadn't been near food for months. Studiously, everyone else ignored him.

"How's Gramma?" Kit asked, changing the subject.

It was Augusta who answered. "I think she's still sleeping. She may have awakened during the night, but if she did she went right back to sleep. I checked on her around two." She set down her cup with meticulous care.

"After your nightmare?" Sally asked. Ignoring Augusta's flush, she added, "There's really no need to worry about Clara. She'll sleep through almost anything. It's you I'm worried about. You can't let yourself become overwrought Augusta, you know that. Tonight I insist you take those pills I brought for you. Obviously the ones you've been taking aren't doing the job any more."

"Have you checked with her doctor?" Kit didn't like to see her aunt taking pills to sleep.

"I'm sure it's all right," Augusta assured Kit. Absently she twisted the cloth napkin by her plate. "After all, Sally is a nurse. If she thinks the pills will help. Oh, dear. I don't know why everyone's making such a fuss. The dream was nothing, nothing at all."

"That's not what Pop thinks, is it Pop?" Lars taunted.

Sally turned to the shrunken old man. "So what *do* you think, Edmund?"

"Ask her," Edmund muttered. "Sounds to me like the same nightmares she had when she went over the edge."

"Nonsense!" said Kit with more force than she intended. "Aunt Augusta, don't listen to all this silly talk. I'm sorry I ever mentioned your nightmare."

"It's all right, Kit." Her aunt sighed. When she got to her feet, her shoulders hunched like those of an elderly woman. "I have to get ready for work now."

She moved slowly to the bathroom while Kit helped Sally clean up. A few minutes later the old woman was gone. A purposeful businesswoman stood in her stead.

After Augusta left for work, Sally went to tend Clara. Avoiding the living room with its uninvited guests, Kit went to the bedroom to read.

"Kit, come here," Sally called.

Sticking her head into her grandmother's warm bedroom, Kit asked, "Did you call me?"

"Yes, dearie, your grandmother wants to talk to you." Sally turned from the bed. "Please don't let her get over tired though."

"I'll try not to. Thanks." Kit limped over and pulled the bench near the bed.

"Kit?"

"I'm here, Gramma."

"I overheard talk of nightmares. Did Augusta have one?"

Not wanting to worry her grandmother, Kit hesitated. "Well...there was some talk at the table last night."

Clara gripped Kit's hand. "Tell me about the nightmare."

"Edmund wanted to know about that, too. Aunt Augusta said it was much like the ones she used to have after her father died, but..."

"Edmund *knows* she had this nightmare?" Her agitation startled Kit.

"Yes, we talked about it at breakfast."

Closing her eyes, Clara fell back against her pillows. "Last night you talked about Claus, *ya*. About his death?"

"We did. I didn't realize until too late how much it still hurt Aunt Augusta. After all, that was years and years ago."

"*Ach*, Kit, you don't understand." The old woman's hands

plucked at the covers. "It is dangerous for Augusta to have those nightmares. It is dangerous for her to remember too much."

Kit tried to calm her grandmother. "I know about her breakdown, but that happened a long time ago. Surely it would be better for Aunt Augusta to accept the past instead of fearing it so much."

Again Clara admonished, "You don't understand. You must stop Augusta from having these nightmares. Don't dig up the past." Clara's faded gaze held Kit's. "I know you're curious about the past. That's only natural, but don't question your aunt. Let me answer any questions you may have. You want to know about your grandfather? It is right. Let me tell you about Claus."

"I don't want to tire you."

"Oh, pooh. I'll talk as long as I like. I am not dead yet, Kit. You of all people should know enough not to let others dictate ridiculous terms just because neither you nor I can get around like everyone else."

Kit grinned. "Maybe you're right, Gramma. I'll stay as long as you want to talk."

Once more Clara closed her eyes. "Claus had a heart condition. One night he asked Augusta to bring his pills. He felt an attack coming on, you see. By the time she returned, it was too late. Claus," Clara said huskily, "My dear Claus was gone. Augusta, naturally enough, blamed herself. Of course it wasn't her fault, but no one could convince her of that. You already know what happened to her, don't you?"

"She had a nervous breakdown."

"*Ya*, she did not come out of it for over a year."

"And she still can't recall what happened that night?"

Clara shook her head. "Somewhere in here, she knows." Clara pointed to her head. "If she tries too hard to remember it may be too much for her. I'm afraid."

"Afraid of what, Gramma?"

Clara turned her head away. "I think I'm tired now, Kit. Will you do one last thing for me?"

"If I can."

"Go upstairs and bring down the photo albums with Claus in them. I would like this, *ya*."

"Sure, Gramma. I'll go up right now and bring them down." Gramma Clara was asleep even before her granddaughter left the room. Only then did Kit remember about the jewelry box. *I'll tell her about it later*, she thought.

Opening the door to the upstairs, Kit gazed in dismay. The steep stairs had no rail for her to lean on. Oh why had her grandmother asked her, rather than her aunt or Sally, to retrieve the photo albums? For them it would be so easy. She hesitated. Maybe she could ask Sally. *No*. Gramma asked her to find them, and she probably had her own reasons for doing so.

Leaning against the wall, Kit carefully tested each step as she ascended the stairs. Panting from exertion, Kit stepped out onto the floor and sighed with relief.

Though unfinished, the upstairs was as neat as the lived in rooms downstairs. The boxes had been neatly shelved and were without a sign of dust or cobwebs. "How like Auntie," said Kit to herself.

On a shelf in the corner, she found several scrapbooks and photo albums. Sliding a heavy box over to the corner, Kit sat down on it and leafed through the albums one by one. She found a whole world of her history she had not known before: pictures of her grandmother Katalina, her grandfather, Clara, her mother, and her aunt. Augusta was actually quite pretty in those days.

As she thumbed through the yellowing pages, one picture caught her eye. It was her aunt beside a handsome young man with a familiar twist to his lips. *Lars?* Lars was much younger than her aunt. The picture couldn't be of him, could it? Her grandfather, Clara's husband then?

Another idea hung just out of reach in her mind. Frowning, Kit turned the page.

CHAPTER SEVEN

"Every purpose is established by counsel:..." Proverbs 20:18a

The albums represented a history filled with secrets, and a past that set her apart from her own family. In a house filled with relatives, Kit felt alone. Something inside yearned for more than photos of persons and places about which she had no personal knowledge.

She wanted the security of a home, the warmth of a loving family. Glancing at her hands as they gripped the photo album, hands that were functional but not in the least appealing, Kit bit her lip unhappily. Would she ever have a home to call her own, or someone to love? Would she ever find someone who loved her despite her limitations and lack of physical perfection?

Wiping away the tears stinging her eyes, Kit forced her thoughts to the project at hand. There was something strange going on in this house and it made her uneasy and insecure. *Lord, please help me. Something is wrong, I feel it. Lord, what—*

"Kit, have you found those albums?" Sally's strident question interrupted Kit's prayer.

"Sally," Kit called down the stairwell. "Is Gramma all right?"

"Aye, dearie, she be askin' for you again."

"Be right down." She glanced down at the digital watch Dr. Ellis presented her with on her last birthday with the dry comment, "Now there'll be no excuse for you to be late for either an appointment or therapy."

She smiled. Two hours had elapsed. Well, no one could accuse her of being late when she had no idea her grandmother would awaken again so soon.

Quickly slamming the album closed, Kit lurched to her feet. She stretched her legs to get them mobile again after sitting cramped for so long. Taking up two other albums, Kit anchored them under her arm before slowly, carefully descending the steep stairs. At the bottom she sighed. *Please, Lord, help me to not have to do those stairs again.*

After catching her breath, Kit took the albums to her grandmother. "How are you feeling, Gramma?"

"A little tired." Clara smiled. "You have found the pictures, *ya*?"

With care, Kit laid one on her grandmother's lap and the rest on the covers beside her. She watched as her grandmother caressed the leather cover before opening it. "Look, Kit. There is Claus. My, was he not handsome! See, I caught him at the plow. You can hardly see his smile for dirt."

Despite the dark smudge across his cheek, Kit had to admit her grandfather was indeed a handsome man. Her chest tightened. Reaching out she touched the picture as though to connect with the past. With a jolt, she realized the man in the picture looked nothing like the picture she thought might be Lars.

Before she could ask about that picture, her grandmother continued. "Look, here's our wedding picture. Don't we look solemn." One by one Clara pored over the pages. "We were so happy then, before..."

"Before he died?"

Clara jumped as Kit spoke. Kit guessed her grandmother had forgotten her presence. "*Ya*," said Clara at last, "before he died."

Her eyelids fluttering, Clara slumped back against pillows she herself had embroidered with fancy designs.

"Gramma, are you all right? Do you want me to get Sally?"

"No dear, not yet. Just regretting an old woman's regrets." Sighing a long deep sigh, she stared at Kit. "Have you ever done anything you wish you could undo?"

"Of course, who hasn't?" Biting her lip, Kit shifted her weight to her other foot as she sought to ease the ache in her legs.

"*Ya*, but for me," Clara spoke softly, "maybe it is too late to make amends. If only you were not involved. Sophia..."

"Gramma is there something you want me to do? Maybe I could do it, just like Mom. After all, you did ask me to come. Please let me help."

Clara patted her granddaughter's hand. "Perhaps. You are much like your mother. You have her inner peace, as well as her strength of character. I wish Augusta..." She shook her head. "Go now. I am too tired to think what to do. Go. We will talk again later."

"What about the albums?"

Her grandmother clutched them against her chest. "No, do not take them. Claus..." Her eyes sank shut. She looked so vulnerable.

Her eyes misty, Kit leaned over and kissed her grandmother's cheek before tiptoeing from the room.

She found Sally in the dining room setting up for the noon meal. "Here let me help. I forgot to tell you at breakfast, but I won't be here for lunch."

"Oh?"

"A...a friend is picking me up." Kit felt her cheeks grow warm.

"How nice for you. I had no idea you had friends here in the city. Is this someone you met when you were at the rehabilitation center here?"

"No, we flew from Kearney together. He's here to attend a conference."

"Oh." Kit didn't know how to interpret the look Sally threw in her direction.

"I'm sorry, I really should have told you earlier. I was so caught up with Gramma."

"Speaking of Clara. I'd better check on her." Sally returned carrying the albums. "You left these on the bed."

"She wouldn't let me take them back," Kit said. "She wanted to remember Claus. I think she wants to go to him."

"Aye, dearie, I think so too. Don't be sad. She's had a long full life." Setting the albums on the edge of the sideboard, Sally leafed through the photos while they conversed.

"I know," Kit said, blinking back tears. "Even though I know she'll be with Claus and Mom, I'll miss her." Kit gripped the back of the nearest chair. She was heartily tired of losing those she cared for.

Sally nodded. "You're religious, too, I can see, dearie. That's good if it gives you comfort."

Kit searched the nurse's face. "You talk as though you don't believe yourself."

The larger woman shrugged. "Death is death as far as I'm concerned. The time to live is now. That's why I believe we have to grab all the happiness possible while we have the chance."

Shaking her head, Kit loosened the grip she had on the dining room chair. "I'm sorry for you, Sally. Though I do believe in living to the fullest here on earth, I don't believe life ends with death. Jesus promised not only some far off paradise, but also peace and strength for each day. He promised He would never forget or forsake us."

She longed to convince Sally, but her own heart accused her. Did she really have any more faith than Sally? God was the one who'd taken away her parents. God was the one who'd failed to answer her prayer for healing...or for love.

Seeing the look on Kit's face Sally asked, "Do you actually believe this yourself? After all you've been through, Kit, do you believe God cares for you?"

"I have a lot of doubts sometimes," Kit admitted. "I'll be the first to admit I don't always understand, but yes, I do believe." Kit, afraid her face revealed just how great those doubts were, reached to align a fork that she found slightly out of place.

Sally shrugged. "That's fine for you, I guess. Let's drop the subject for now, all right?"

Kit turned back in relief. "Where's Lars? Did he and Edmund leave?"

"Edmund's still in the living room turning that infernal hourglass end over end. Gets on my nerves. When I look at him now it's hard to imagine the debonair young man I once knew."

"Clara said he was quite handsome."

"He was also bullheaded, stubborn, and always getting into trouble...from which his sister was always extricating him." Sally's eyes flashed.

"I suppose you knew him from way back."

"You forget I grew up around the family. My folks were the outsiders in an otherwise Swedish settlement, which made it hard sometimes. Back then the Swedes really believed Swedish was the language of heaven." Sally laughed, but Kit heard bitterness in her laughter.

"Clara was different. She was always nice to me. She let me earn money by helping around the house. Yes, dearie, I was around. I knew a lot of what went on."

"Are you saying you were around when Edmund came to America?" Kit leaned forward.

Sally hesitated a moment. "I went with the family to pick him up. He tried to settle down. He married and had Lars. One morning, before Lars was scarce out of diapers, Edmund woke up to find his wife gone. She ran off with some other man. I'm afraid Edmund wasn't the fatherly type, so I tried to help him out with Lars."

"You don't like them very much, do you?"

"Maybe I know him too well." Sally's heavy shoulders lifted and she made a face. "They're stubborn and none too bright, but they can be led." She shook her head. "Edmund never was much of a man, for all his handsome looks, and Lars is even worse."

"Sounds like you knew Edmund pretty well."

"I should," Sally said. "I was in his house often enough taking care of the two of them. For awhile, he and I thought of making our arrangement permanent."

"You and Uncle Edmund?"

Sally laughed. "Hard to believe, isn't it? Remember this was a long time ago. He wasn't so bad then." Sally slapped the albums shut before shuffling her bulk into the kitchen.

Kit knew she'd get no more out of Sally for the time being. Thoughtfully, she retired to her bedroom to freshen up her make up and comb her hair once more before going into the living room to wait for Dr. Long.

She almost hated sitting down in the same room where her uncle waited, hunched in his chair, turning that infernal hourglass over and over until she wanted to scream. The sneer on Lars' face as he watched her made her skin crawl. Impatiently she watched the clock on the mantel with almost as much intensity as her uncle watched his hourglass. When a knock sounded at the door, she rushed to the door as fast as she was able. She well knew neither her uncle nor Lars would stir.

"Dr. Long!" Staring up at him, Kit noticed his size all over again, the dark hair across his forehead and the penetrating gray eyes that seemed to hold concern. "Dr. Long," she said again as relief washed over her. She swayed against the doorframe.

***

Keith reached for her arm, as though to assure himself she was real. "Are you all right?" He felt her tremble beneath his hand and frowned.

She smiled. "It's nothing. I'm fine. Please...come in and meet everyone."

Keith, following her into the house, noted the faces of the two men who sat in the dark room.

Edmund roused himself only enough to ask, "You a real doctor?"

"A doctor?" Lars laughed. "Is my dear cousin one of your patients? I didn't think she was so bad off she needed a house call."

"I'm a psychologist, not an orthopedist," Keith said. His hand on Kit's arm tightened protectively.

Lars rolled his eyes. "So Kit, are you as crazy as Cousin Augusta?"

Crimson staining her cheeks, Kit bit her lip. Keith felt her embarrassment and placed a comforting hand against the small of her back. More than anything, he wanted to whisk Kit away from her unpleasant relatives. With difficulty he remained calm. "I'm a friend of Kit's," he said, adding slowly, "A good friend."

Lars shrugged. Turning the hourglass over, Edmund ignored them. Keith felt hate, tension, and fear coiling itself like a python about the room, gradually tightening its hold. He felt Kit tremble and drew her closer to him.

"Nice meeting you both," he said, "but we must be going. Kit, are you ready?"

"Oh, yes," she said. Relief flashed in her eyes as she picked up her purse. "I'm ready."

Without further ceremony, Keith hustled her from the gloomy house to his car. How could a sensitive woman like Kit stand living there even temporarily? His lips tightened. After what he'd just seen of her family, he intended to make sure she enjoyed herself this afternoon.

Frowning, he drove along silently. As they left her grandmother's house further and further behind, he watched Kit relax. She lay her head against the cushioned headrest, and her hands unclenched on her lap.

"Been pretty awful?" he finally asked. Glancing at her, he watched her tense again.

"Yes. It was different when I came for treatment at the rehabilitation center seven years ago." She took a deep breath. "Thanks for coming to my rescue. I didn't realize how much I needed to get away for awhile."

"My specialty is rescuing pretty damsels in distress." Reaching over he tucked a stray lock of hair behind her ear.

He watched her eyes widen, then sparkle with tears before she turned to stare out the window. He heard her murmur of surprise, "Pretty?" and felt anger simmer deep inside. Didn't she know?

"You are pretty, you know," he drawled, not looking at her.

Silence. Finally she asked, "Where are we headed?"

"Anoka."

"Isn't that quite a ways?"

"Thirty miles or so. You'll love it. Beth has a new home right beside the Mississippi River." He went on to describe the two-story rustic house surrounded by ash, birch and pine.

"Sounds lovely. I can't wait to see it. You sure your sister doesn't mind?"

"No. She's much more gregarious than I am."

Silence fell again. Kit watched the scenery whiz by. Cars honked and juggled for position. Tall buildings gave place to long, flat ones, large mansions to cozy homes, businesses to a stretch of countryside that made Kit think of home. She found herself thinking of her conversation with Sally, and wishing she was as sure of her faith as she had tried to sound.

"Dr. Long."

"Keith. My name is Keith." He quirked an eyebrow. "Unless you prefer Mr. Spock?"

As he probably intended, Kit smiled. "I'll have to think about that, Dr. Long." At his mock look of exasperation, she said, "All right...Keith."

"That's better. Now, what is it?"

"I was talking with Sally earlier."

Keith spared her a glance. "Who's Sally?"

"That's right, you didn't meet her. She's Gramma's nurse...and an old friend of the family. Well, she was questioning my belief that God loves and cares for us. In fact, I'm not even sure she believes in God."

"But you do?"

Kit hesitated. "When I tried to sound convincing about my own faith, I realized...I realized..." She turned to look at him. "I'm not so sure God really does care about me." Her shoulders tensed.

"Lars treats me like I'm some kind of leper. I know the Bible says God accepts me as I am, but sometimes I wonder if Jesus feels the same way about me as Lars does...repulsed. Sometimes I wonder if I've done something so awful He can't love me. Why else would He take both my mother and father away when I needed them so much? Why else would He leave me like this?" She held up her hands.

Keith glanced at her, his eyes dark with compassion. "Kit...."

Now that she started, years of questioning, hurt and pain tumbled out. "Do you know how badly I wanted a date when I was in college? Sure, I had lots of friends and we did things together. The young men either treated me like a sister, someone to listen to them about their problems with girlfriends or classes, or else like a child who needed cosseting. Others..." Kit shrugged.

"Rejected you because of your physical impairment."

Staring blindly out the window, Kit nodded. "At times I think I must have failed God. Then again, I get mad at Him for failing me! I love Him, truly I do, but..." Falling silent, Kit gulped back tears. Why had she said so much? What would Keith think of her now?

Reaching over, Keith squeezed her arm. "So you've been afraid not only of loving and trusting God, but anyone else as well."

Kit gasped. "How did you know that?"

"Your feelings aren't uncommon." As though sensing her hurt, Keith appeared to consider his words carefully. She sensed a genuine interest in helping her. "Tell me," he said at last, "what horrible thing have you done to make God turn His back on you?"

"That's just it, I don't know. I've thought and thought about it, but—"

"Do you know that verse about Satan being the accuser of the brethren?"

"Y...es."

"Kit I think you've been listening to the accuser's voice, not God's. You've let yourself be filled with doubt because you're hurt, and you don't understand how a good God could allow such things to happen to you. Am I right?"

Kit mulled it over. "Maybe," she said cautiously, "but why...?"

"Has God ever really failed you? Think about it. When your parents died, were you left without friends or people to help you?"

"No. There was Dr. Ellis, and Ruth, and lots of people from the church. They brought in meals, cleaned the apartment, and did lots of things to help out."

"As for being physically disabled, don't you think God loves all those other people who suffer with some sort of physical pain or limitation? You're not the only person who lives with a disability, you know."

"Oh, but I have been healed!"

"How's that?" Keith turned to stare at her.

"Dad took me to some revival meetings in Texas some years after I got sick. They were wonderful, and they prayed for the sick."

"You were prayed for?" Keith's voice sounded skeptical.

Kit nodded. "It was unbelievable. All these people sought help, yet the evangelist looked at me and said, 'I've seen you sitting in the aisle day after day. The Lord told me to pray especially for you tonight, and that's what I'm going to do.'"

"So you were healed?" Kit noted the cynical twist to his lips.

"Yes...and no. Later it was just another thing that made me wonder if God really loved me. But at the time, I felt surrounded by so much love. The man prayed and suddenly all the pain left my body. It was as though a key unlocked a door inside me. For the first time in years, I felt well and strong inside.

"Outside though, nothing had changed. But, from that moment on, I began to improve. I didn't need as many painkillers anymore, and I got stronger. Still I felt God let me down. I couldn't understand why he'd take the pain away but leave me like this." She spread her gnarled fingers on her lap.

"Someone, I don't recall who, said God healed me of the disease, but He didn't restore what the disease had destroyed. I wanted Him to do it all. He could...but He didn't. I didn't want to go back to the doctors. But," she hesitated for a moment before continuing, "Some individuals told me my faith wasn't strong enough. That made me so mad, for awhile, I didn't even want to believe in God. But I do. I've had so many doubts, but felt uncomfortable about them. Admitting my faith isn't as great as it should be is really hard."

Reaching over, Keith squeezed her hand. His tone gentle, he said, "So you've been afraid to confide in anyone. You've been afraid they'd judge you for your feelings. You were afraid they'd let you down, too."

Kit's eyes burned. "I don't know why I'm telling you all this now." Staring out the window to keep him from seeing her blink back tears, she asked, "Do you think I'm silly?"

"No, I don't. I think you've been through a lot and your feelings are perfectly understandable. But think of all God *has* done for you. He gave you a good friend in Dr. Ellis. Do you realize there are no lengths to which that man wouldn't go to just to keep you walking? He thinks the world of you. And Ruth...ever since I came to the clinic, I've heard her talk about how wonderful you are. As for your parents, though they're gone now, you were blessed to have them while you were growing up. Not everyone has the security of loving parents."

"That's true."

"You have a place to live, food to eat, a church body who cares about you, and friends. Do you know how rare that combination is in this world?"

"I never thought about it in just that way." Kit hung her head. When she raised her head, tears shone in her eyes. "God hasn't failed me. I've failed Him. I've failed Him miserably." The tears pricking her eyes began running down her cheeks as the hard knot inside melted away.

All this time she'd held the hurt inside, let it eat away at her, let it undermine her faith and trust in her Heavenly Father. Keith made it all so simple.

He tightened his grip on her hand. The warmth of his touch spread to her heart; for he touched her not with revulsion, but with tenderness. "Don't let rejection turn you against God, Kit. Remember they even rejected Christ when he was on earth. The opinions of others don't matter, not to God. He loves you. He cares about you." He hesitated a moment, then said firmly, "I care, too, Kit, very much."

Through her tears, Kit stared at him. "What did you say?"

His smile melted a cold place inside. "You heard me. I care

about you, Kit." He paused, his eyebrow raising. "And not just as my Christian duty, either. All right?"

As he probably intended, Kit quirked him a watery smile. "All right."

"Good. Now, don't you have a tissue to wipe those tears?"

Pulling several tissues from her purse, Kit wiped her face and blew her nose. Though she felt like a child, she was too happy to care. She glanced toward Keith. "Would you mind if we prayed?"

"Of course not."

Kit bowed her head. She felt embarrassed, but felt she really needed to confess her fears and doubts not only God, but also to Keith. "Lord Jesus, forgive me for not trusting you. Forgive me for not recognizing your love, and for refusing to believe you love me. Because I felt rejected, I rejected you. Forgive me. Please help me to trust you. Thank you for loving me even when I've been afraid to love you or...anyone else. Amen."

Beside her Keith's deep voice reverberated in the car, startling Kit. "Father, thank you for helping Kit see how much you love her. Please be with her during this difficult time with her grandmother. Give her strength and patience, Lord. And," he hesitated. "Thank you for bringing Kit into my life. In Christ's name, amen."

Lifting her head, Kit smiled at Keith through fresh tears...healing tears.

"Feel any better?"

"It's like a load off my heart," Kit said simply. "Thank you...friend." Leaning back she found a silly grin on her face. She hadn't felt so free, or so unencumbered, since before she got ill. How could she thank Keith for that? Or God!

***

Keith was right; she loved his sister's rustic house. Here on the outskirts of the huge metropolis, the wide Mississippi meandered by the peaceful oasis where virtually untouched forests surrounded sloping, green lawns.

He was right, too, about her welcome. His plump, matronly sister enveloped her in large, welcoming arms. "So this is little Kit. I'm so glad to meet you, dear. I'm eager to know all about you. You know how Keith is. Getting information out him is like prying open a clam." Beth's chatter as she ushered her into the living room, eased the tension and made Kit feel at home.

"My husband, John, is at work," Beth told her. "And Lisa, that's our oldest, is a counselor at camp this year. Heidi should be here for lunch, though she wasn't sure what she and her friend, Sheila, were going to do."

Beth motioned toward the large, comfortable corner sofa that took up much of the living room. "Sit down. Sit down. I'll have lunch on in a few minutes."

"I'd like to show Kit the view from the porch," said Keith holding out his hand. With only the slightest of hesitations, Kit slipped her hand into his. Her pulse raced as his large hand enclosed hers.

When he smiled down at her, she feared her knees would give way. "Okay." It came out as a squeak.

"Okay, just okay?" he teased. Clasping her hand more tightly, he led her through sliding glass doors to the redwood deck overlooking the lawns and the river.

Awed by the breathtaking sight, Kit leaned against the railing. Below her a small building seemed to float on the water next to the dock.

"That's the boathouse." Keith said. "And that," he pointed out the sleek cruiser tied up at the dock, "is John's boat. After dinner I'd like to take you out for a spin."

"Oh, Keith," Kit exclaimed, "it's beautiful out here! I—" At that moment a young girl of perhaps thirteen ran through the door, followed by another girl of about the same age. "Uncle Keith!"

"Heidi." Keith smiled fondly at his niece. "Come here. Meet my friend, Kit."

Heidi surveyed Kit with the curiosity of youth, then smiled a welcome as genuine as her mother's. "Glad ta meet you, Kit." She glanced toward her uncle. "Uncle Keith, are you taking her for a boat ride after lunch?"

"Those are my plans." Tugging on Heidi's braid, he asked, "I don't suppose you and your friend would like to tag along, now would you?"

Flipping her long, dark braid out of his reach, Heidi grinned. "Someone has to chaperone you."

Catching Kit's gaze, Keith winked. She felt color flood her cheeks. "Hmm...maybe I'll have to rethink my offer."

"Too late, Uncle Keith. We'll be ready."

"Heidi, Sheila, please come here." Beth called the girls to help her set out platters of food and pitchers of lemonade. A few minutes later they all sat down on the cushioned redwood chairs around the shaded table. Beth had amply provided fried chicken, coleslaw, potato salad, homemade bread and jam, along with apple pie topped with ice cream.

When they were finished, Keith leaned back and patted his stomach. "Better than the Colonel's, sis. I'll have to do a lot of exercise to wear this off or I'll soon be as fat as a hog." The girls giggled.

Getting to his feet, he asked, "Coming with us, Beth?"

"Sorry, Keith. I have a meeting this afternoon at church. I'll just clean up and leave." She smiled at Kit. "I hope you enjoy yourself this afternoon."

"Oh, I already am," Kit answered. "Thank you for this delicious meal."

After they all helped Beth clear the table, Heidi ran to get the keys for the boat. Excitedly, she and her friend scrambled down the path in front of Keith and Kit.

Taking Kit's hand, Keith helped her down the steps to the curving flagstone path leading to the dock. He matched his long strides to her short, limping ones. When she tried to let go of his hand, he held on more firmly as though unwilling to release her. He held her hand as though he wanted to, not because she needed the assistance. Joy bubbled up inside her at being alive and with someone she cared about.

The sun sparkled on the shiny blue and silver boat. Fluffy clouds drifted slowly across the blue sky. The refrain rang in Kit's head. *God's in His Heaven, all's right with the world*. She wasn't sure she quoted it correctly or where exactly she'd heard the phrase, but today it fit.

The younger girls, already attired in lifejackets, giggled as Keith picked up Kit to set her carefully into the boat. Surely she only imagined his hands lingered on her waist as he set her down.

She stared in dismay at the jacket he handed her. "Sorry," she said, "I haven't the faintest idea how to put it on."

"Don't worry about it. I'll help you." Helping Kit into her jacket, Keith tied the ties with quiet efficiency. Every time their hands touched, Kit felt a jolt clear to her toes and wondered if Keith felt it as well. She sighed in relief when he took his place behind the wheel and edged the boat out into the river.

Suddenly the boat roared to life and the girls squealed as water sprayed over them. Trailing their hands in the water, the giggling girls ignored both Keith and Kit.

Keith, concentrating on his driving, didn't notice when Kit began sliding off the seat. Her hands flayed as she tried to find something to grasp. She tried to brace herself with her feet, but she kept sliding. "Keith," she gasped.

To her embarrassment, he all but scooped her up from the

floor and set her in front of him. His arms held her trembling body close. "Better?"

"Much better. Thanks." Gradually Kit relaxed. Water sprayed into her face, and she turned to catch it full on.

"Having fun?" Keith asked. His breath tickled her ear.

Laughing as the spray drenched her cheeks, Kit nodded. She told herself her exhilaration resulted from the excitement of the ride, and not from the warm touch of Keith's arms around her.

Still, the roar of the engine, and the constant rocking of the boat proved tiring. When at last Keith nudged the boat to the dock, Kit was glad it was over.

"Thanks," called the girls over their shoulders as they ran back to the house to change.

After tying up the boat, Keith lifted Kit out and set her on the ground. She swayed; her legs felt like rubber. Laughing, he picked her up once more and strode up the hill to the porch. "This disability of yours has some advantages after all," he said, gazing down at her.

She glanced up. "What do you mean?"

"Never mind," he said almost gruffly. Once on the porch, he set her down and steadied her until she regained her balance. Taking her hand, he led her back through the sliding doors and on into the kitchen.

Making himself at home, Keith raided the refrigerator for leftover chicken and salad. "I'm hungry," he said. "What about you?"

Normally Kit didn't have much of an appetite, but her hunger surprised her. "Sounds good. I can't believe I'm so hungry after that lunch we had."

"Good for you." Keith surveyed her solemnly. "I hope you had a good afternoon, Kit. In fact I wish I could get you to stay longer, but unfortunately I have a dinner meeting I can't miss."

Kit colored. "Please. I've had a wonderful afternoon. You've done so much for me. I just can't thank you enough." She stumbled about for words to express what she felt.

Keith squeezed her hand and pulled her closer. "I'm glad I could help." He paused. "Did you hear the girls talking about me taking them to ValleyFair in the next day or two?" He surveyed Kit's face until she felt the heat creep into her cheeks again. "Want to come along?"

"Keith, I know you haven't seen a very good side of my family, but I'm doing fine at the house. Really. You don't have to go out of your way to entertain me." She paused, her voice low. "Besides, I don't want to be a nuisance."

"A nuisance? Don't be silly. I want you to come. If I know Heidi and her friend, they'll desert me as soon as I pass the amusement park gate. After I pay for their tickets, I probably won't see them again until it's time to go home. You'd be doing me a favor."

"You sure you wouldn't rather ask someone else to go with you? I know you told Dr. Ellis you'd watch out for me, but—"

"I don't want anyone else." Keith scowled. "If you won't go, I'll go alone. You really don't want that now, do you?"

Though he kept his tone light, Keith realized he meant what he said. He really did want Kit to go with him...and no one else would do. After this afternoon, he knew he had to see her again.

He left Kit, still smiling, in her grandmother's hallway.

Driving to the conference, he tried to reflect on his afternoon with Kit but all he could think about was her soft warmth as he held her in his arms. Somehow his list of "standards" for a wife seemed to pale in comparison to the image of Kit's spray-washed face and sparkling eyes.

CHAPTER EIGHT

"But as for me, this secret is not revealed to me..." Daniel 2:30a

By the time the click-click of Augusta's heels telegraphed her presence on the floor of the kitchen linoleum, Kit, already dressed for dinner, met her with a smile. "How was work?"

Taking off her hat, Augusta poured herself a cup of coffee and sank gratefully onto a kitchen chair. She took a long slow swallow of the dark liquid before answering. "Work? It was fine but exhausting, and the bus connections not the best. I'm late, aren't I?" She twisted to check the clock. "You haven't held dinner long, I trust?" She paused, and sipped her coffee. "So, what did you do today, Katalina?"

"I went out for awhile."

Augusta sat down her cup with a clatter. "Kit. Surely you know how dangerous it is for a young woman to wander alone on these streets...even in this neighborhood. This isn't a small town like you're used to."

Kit smiled. "I wasn't alone, Aunt Augusta. A friend of mine picked me up. We had a picnic at his sister's in Anoka."

"This was someone you knew?" Augusta eyed Kit doubtfully. "Not some stranger you picked up?"

"Of course not. I was with Dr. Long, Keith, who flew with me to Minneapolis. His sister lives here, in Anoka, I mean. Since he has a conference in town this week, my orthopedist sort of put me in his charge." She grimaced at the memory. "I assure you he is eminently trustworthy."

"I suppose it's all right then." Augusta fingered her cup nervously. "Then again, one never knows whom one can trust these days. I'm just glad you're all right." Her aunt took her cup to the sink. "I'll get changed for dinner."

Kit followed her to the bedroom to retrieve her book. Augusta shuddered at the lurid jacket cover with the dead man laid out on the floor. "Doesn't much improve your mind. I have some good books you might read. Billy Graham, Charles Swindoll, Dobson."

"I know, Aunt Augusta. I like reading those books too, but sometimes I just like a good mystery."

Again her aunt glanced at the picture on the cover and shuddered. "I-I'd rather not see that again. Please?"

One look at her aunt's pale face and Kit realized the picture on the cover reminded Augusta of her father's death. Kit tucked the cover out of sight. "I'm sorry. I'll keep it out of your way."

Accidentally bumping into the edge of the dresser, Augusta disturbed the photo albums someone placed there. Augusta eyed them with some agitation. "I haven't seen these in years." Gingerly she flipped one open. Shuddering, she closed it with a snap. "If you'll leave me, Kit, I'll dress."

Kit frowned, wondering why the albums seemed to bother her aunt so much. "About the albums—"

"Did you bring them in here?"

"No," Kit said. "I guess Sally must have moved them here. I—"

Augusta shook her head as though she didn't want to think

about them. "Not now, Kit. I'll just bring them out when I'm finished here."

With a shrug, Kit left her aunt. *Why did the albums seem to disturb her so much?*

After dressing for the evening, Augusta came into the dining room carrying the albums. Lars, already seated at the table, reached for one. "What are these?" he asked as Augusta and Kit sat down.

"Hey, look at this!" Lars drew their attention. "Isn't that my old man under that fancy mustache?"

"Yes...yes, that's Uncle Edmund." Augusta spoke uneasily. "I found them on my dresser. By the way, Kit, who brought these down from the attic? And why?"

"I did," answered Kit. "Gramma asked me to." She caught a haunted look in her aunt's eyes.

"Surely Mother knew better than to send you, of all people, up those steep stairs." Shaking her head, Augusta added firmly, "I'll take them right back up where they belong. Mother must be more confused than I thought."

"Maybe she knew I could do it," Kit defended her grandmother. "I did, too. The steps were solid and I was careful."

"Yes...of course." Kit had the distinct impression Augusta implied something more than Kit's disability.

"Well, I suppose it's too late to take them up now." Closing the album, Augusta reached to put it on the sideboard. Lars topped it with his. "Don't take them back, Kit," she instructed her niece. "Let me see to that. I don't see why Mother wanted these old things dragged down anyway."

Kit softened her retort to, "Seeing pictures of Claus made Gramma happy. That's reason enough."

"Mother. How is she?" Augusta leaped to her feet. "I should have checked on her first thing. And where is Sally? Is something wrong? Oh, what was the matter with me? How could I forget?"

"Auntie," Kit put her hand on her aunt's arm. "Gramma's fine. And when you were late, I helped Sally get supper ready. Don't worry. Sally's with Gramma, but she'll be out any minute."

"Augusta. Good you're home." As Sally bustled into the dining room, Augusta sank back into the chair.

"And Mother?"

"No change, Augusta. Now don't worry your head." Sally marched into the kitchen.

Over dinner, Sally kept up a stream of cheerful conversation. The meal was more pleasant than the night before, but Kit couldn't help but compare it to the light and happy conversation around Beth's picnic table. Lars and Edmund carried an atmosphere of dark bitterness with them, and Kit was relieved when the meal ended.

While Kit helped Sally clear the table, Lars and Edmund shuffled back into the living room. Lips pressed together, Augusta picked up the albums. She headed out the arched door of the dining room into the small hall that connected both bedrooms, the bath, and the entryway to the stairs. "I'm taking these back upstairs," she said.

Sorry she hadn't had more time to examine the albums further, Kit followed Sally into the kitchen.

She had just picked up a dishtowel when a scream rent the air, followed by a thump-thumpety-thump-thud. Exchanging a stunned glance with Sally, Kit threw down the towel and limped quickly through the dining room to the hall where the door to the stairs hung open. "Sally, come on! Something's happened to Aunt Augusta!"

She found her aunt lying dazed at the bottom of the stairs, her left foot turned under at a strange angle. Gently Sally probed the ankle. "Does it hurt?"

Wincing, Augusta nodded.

"I don't think it's broken. Here." Putting her arms around

Augusta's thin shoulders, Sally helped her to her feet. "Lean on me, dearie."

Frustrated at her inability to help, Kit watched the broad nurse practically drag her aunt to the bedroom. This was one of those times when her disability most frustrated her, and when she felt the most useless. Tears of self-pity sprang to her eyes and her mind automatically turned to her usual accusations. Abruptly, she recalled her conversation with Keith.

Jesus loved her. He loved her enough to die for her, and to provide her with those who loved her. No, she would not let that hurt grow in her again. Job came to mind. He lost his family, just like her, but he still trusted. He lost his health, like her, but he still trusted. He lost everything he had, yet he still trusted. In the end, God rewarded his faithfulness.

He trusted through calamities much worse than her own. Surely she could trust as well. Again she felt peace spread like balm within. The corners of her lips turned up even as she swiped tears from her eyes.

The albums, half open, lay scattered on the stairs. Straining, Kit was able to grasp and close them. Shifting them in her arms, she decided to check on her grandmother.

Had Augusta's scream disturbed her? How could it not? Yet Augusta's scream the night before didn't wake her. Opening the door, Kit tiptoed in to her grandmother's room. Silently she put the albums on the dresser, then tiptoed to the door. Hesitating she turned back, waiting for Clara's chest to rise and fall. Was it natural for her to sleep so deeply? Sally said she'd begin to sleep more and more.

With a sigh, Kit limped into her aunt's bedroom. Sally had Augusta spread out on the bed, her leg elevated and her ankle covered with a cold pack. "How is it?" asked Kit.

"She'll be fine, dearie. I'm pretty sure it's only a sprain."

"She'll need x-rays, won't she?"

"X-rays!" Augusta moaned.

"Now Augusta." Sally patted her arm. "Don't get all worked up. Kit was only making a suggestion, weren't you dearie?" Her eyes narrowed as she stared at Kit.

"I just thought—"

"Like I said," Sally interrupted before Kit could finish, "it's only a sprain, Augusta. But if it would make you feel better, I'll see you get to the doctor for x-rays."

Augusta fell back against the pillows. "Sally, you said it was only a sprain." She turned to Kit. "Sally is never wrong about these things."

Kit bit her lip to keep herself from arguing. "How do you feel, Aunt Augusta?"

Augusta, her face pale, looked like a crumpled rag doll. "I just don't understand it. I've been up and down those steps a thousand times."

Sally adjusted the cold compress on Augusta's raised ankle. "Now Augusta, I don't want you fretting about this. Accidents happen. Maybe an x-ray would make you feel better."

Shaking her head, Augusta said, "I can't. I have to go to work in the morning. You did say it was only sprained. I must go to work!" Panic flashed in her eyes.

Kit protested, "One day of sick leave surely won't hurt you."

"No. No. No! I haven't missed a day for illness in twenty years. No, I mustn't miss work."

"Well then," Kit said, "you must have lots of sick leave built up."

Augusta choked, "When mother...goes, I'll take it. I'll need it then, not now. Please?"

Sally pressed her lips tightly together. Hands on her wide hips, she stared down at Augusta. "I think you'd better have those x-rays after all. I'll not be havin' anyone say I didn't do my best for you." She glanced at Kit. "Now, I'll get you pills for the pain and those other pills to help you sleep. Tonight you will take them." Once more she turned to Kit. "Please see that she takes them."

Kit hesitated. "I'll remind her."

Sally's forehead creased with concern. "Maybe I should stay over."

"No, not on my account," Augusta protested. "Besides, I have no bed to offer you."

Sally sighed. "Well, all right, but you must promise to call me if you need me...even in the middle of the night."

"Mother?"

"Kit can look in on her. If either of you need me, I can be here in under half an hour."

Relieved, Augusta smiled. "Thank you, Sally. You've always been a good friend."

Leaving the two older women alone, Kit drifted through the hall, into the dining room, and through the large arched doorway into the living room. Edmund stared at her; his eyes glittered in the light of the lamp. "What happened?" he demanded.

"Aunt Augusta fell." Turning at a rude sound emanating from somewhere behind her, Kit caught the sardonic grin on her cousin's face.

"Old lady should be more careful of the stairs," he snorted.

Thoughtfully, Kit searched his face. "I didn't say she fell on the stairs. How did you know?"

Lars shrugged. "From all the racket she made, a deaf man could have told you that."

Kit shook her head in disgust. "Then why didn't you try to help her?"

Nonchalantly, Lars shrugged again. "That's what Sally's paid for. The old biddy should know better than to climb those dangerous stairs."

"Dangerous! I was on those stairs just this morning. They were steep, yes, but not otherwise dangerous."

"Well good for you. Just goes to show the old girl's even more tottery than I thought."

Letting out a breath in exasperation, Kit fled back to the bedroom. "Is Sally with Gramma?" she asked her aunt.

Her aunt nodded. "Yes, she's getting her ready for the night."

Kit sat on the edge of Augusta's bed. "Feeling any better?"

"I'm fine, but," Augusta clenched and unclenched her hands. "It's strange. Katalina. I am almost sure one of those steps gave way under me. And to think you went up them. If you had fallen..."

Kit didn't much like the image Augusta presented to her mind. "Listen, Auntie. When I went up those steps, they were solid. Every one of them. Believe me, I checked."

Augusta shook her head. "It doesn't make any sense. I did *not* slip. At least, I don't think I did." Her voice wavered. "I was so sure it was the step. Yet you say—"

"Wait!" Kit stood up. "Let me check." Going to the stairs, she swung open the narrow door. In the dim light, she surveyed the steps. Halfway to the top, a single board hung lose. It swung from a nail. Her stomach lurched. Augusta's fall had not been an accident!

She had an overwhelming impulse to call Keith. How she longed for the security of his arms. No, of course, she couldn't bother him. Besides she had no idea where he might be tonight. Still the thought persisted.

What is going on? Kit leaned against the doorframe, her fingers gripping the wood until her knuckles turned white. *Oh, Lord, help me know what to do*!

CHAPTER NINE

He that...layeth up deceit within him; When he speaketh fair,
believe him not. Proverbs 26:24-25a

Thoughts whirled in Kit's head. The loose board frightened her. Those steps had been solid just this morning. Clasping her hands nervously in a dismaying imitation of her aunt, Kit fought against the panic welling inside her as she struggled with the thought that wouldn't go away. Someone tampered with the step in a deliberate attempt to injure or to scare someone.

Was the sabotage meant for her, or her aunt? Why? Who wanted to do harm to either of them? As far as she could tell, Aunt Augusta was harmless enough. As for herself...Kit forced a smile at the idea someone might see her as a threat.

Her smile faded and Kit shuddered. If she had taken the albums up those stairs, she could have been killed. Her aunt's fall had been bad enough, but Kit wouldn't have been able to break her own fall at all. She groaned out loud, aching to call Keith. Her heart pounded. Right now she needed the comfort of his calming presence.

Gulping down her fear, Kit closed her eyes. She visualized the enigmatic visage of the tall doctor. Mentally she explained her suspicions to him.

He raised his eyebrow. "Have you proof, any proof at all?"

"Not really," she whispered, "but—"

"Are you certain your fears don't stem from your overactive imagination? After all, at this moment you're in the middle of an imaginary conversation."

Kit sighed. No, she had nothing but conjecture. As much as she'd like to, she just could *not* run to Keith with her vague suspicions.

It suddenly occurred to her that despite having known Keith a scant few days, she thought of him a great deal. Relying on him so heavily was probably not healthy. He wasn't available, but God was.

"Lord," she whispered. "Help me to rely on you. What should I do? Who can I tell?"

Should she go to her grandmother? Definitely not. Augusta then? No, it would only upset her further. Certainly she couldn't go to either Uncle Edmund or Lars. She imagined the scorn in Lars' voice. Lars! Kit stiffened. Would Lars do such a thing? Yes, Kit decided he would if he had enough reason. But what reason could he, or anyone else, possibly have?

Who else could she confide in? Of course, Sally! Kit sighed with relief as Sally, closing the door behind her, exited Gramma Clara's bedroom. "Sally, come here. I want to show you something." Kit pointed out the broken step. "That was solid this morning."

Hands on her hips, Sally surveyed the stairs. "My, that does look wicked, dearie."

"That's why Augusta fell, Sally."

Sally shook her head. "Someone should have checked those stairs before now. They've probably been loosening up for sometime."

"No, I told you," said Kit, "All those steps were perfectly fine this morning when I went up them. I tested each one."

"More than likely you had a lucky escape, dearie." Sally's eyes narrowed as she glanced from the stairs to Kit and back again. "How could the step be solid this morning, when by the time your aunt stepped on it, it obviously wasn't? That doesn't make any sense, does it?"

Realizing there was no use arguing, Kit bit her lip to keep herself from accusing anyone. Helplessly she stared at the broken step.

Sympathetically Sally patted Kit's shoulder. "This has been a shock for you, dearie. You've had nothing but problems since you came. There's Clara's illness, then the behavior of those ghouls Edmund and Lars, Augusta's nightmares, now this frightful accident. You must realize this was just that...an accident." Her gaze rested on Kit's pale face. "You're not letting your imagination run away with you, are you dearie?"

Kit shrugged and turned toward her room. "Thanks, Sally. I guess I just needed to talk to someone about it."

Sally's broad face creased into a smile. "I'm always ready to listen, dearie. But it's late, and time for me to get on home. If you're sure you're all right?"

Kit sighed. "Yes, I'm fine."

Sally headed toward the back door. "Oh, by the way, Kit. Make sure Augusta takes her pills."

"I'll remind her," Kit said, but didn't quite meet Sally's gaze.

"Well then, good-bye dearie. See you tomorrow." Kit heard the back door close and Sally's little car start up in the back drive.

Partly to make sure Augusta didn't try to go to work, Sally returned earlier than usual the next morning.

"Forget about going to work, Augusta," she said. "I've already called the doctor. You have an appointment this morning to get that ankle checked."

Her aunt made little protest as Sally helped her toward the door. Kit planned to spend the morning visiting with her grandmother, but Sally forestalled her. Glancing back over her shoulder, the nurse called, "Clara's very tired this morning. Please don't disturb her."

Reluctantly, Kit nodded.

After they left, loneliness smothered Kit. In the hot muggy air, her short-sleeved red top clung to her. The thought of sitting in the gloomy living room drove her to the bedroom where, with a disappointing sigh, she finished her book. She slammed it closed in frustration.

"Lord, why am I here anyway? No one but Gramma really wants me here and I've scarcely seen her. What am I to do? And what about the jewelry box?"

Hearing the front door squeak open, Kit walked into the living room in time to see Lars amble in and fling himself down onto the couch. "When's breakfast ready?"

"Get it yourself." She felt no guilt over her rudeness. "Sally has taken Aunt Augusta to the doctor."

Edmund shuffled in and sat down. "Come talk to an old man," he whined.

Fervently wishing she'd never left the bedroom, Kit pulled out the piano bench and perched on its edge. The old man's glittering gaze rested on her face. A crafty smile curled his lips and sent shivers down Kit's spine.

Something about that smile sent a flood of memories through her mind, memories of pain and humiliation she'd tried hard to forget. The memories of one hospital after another, one rehabilitation center after another blended together with the sometimes quiet, sometimes strident half-remembered voices of the nurses.

Though she tried to push away the past, Edmund's expression reminded her of the rehab center that had left her with nightmares for months. She recalled the sly gaze of the drunken porter who had smashed her aching body, more than once, against the wall. It reminded her, too, of experimental medicines that made her constantly feel ill, and of careless attendants who ignored the patients' buzzers, leaving them screaming in pain.

There were other, more humane centers, but each left a scar on her soul and a question of her own self worth.

Each venture started with the promise of walking again, and ended with so much pain, frustration, humiliation and despair. With each failure to improve, her conviction grew that God did not love her.

Taking a deep breath, Kit closed the door against her painful memories. God loved her. Hadn't he rescued her from those horrors, brought her to Kearney, and Dr. Ellis' clinic? Thanks to Dr. Ellis, she now walked. His clinic was so different. The first time she'd walked in, she'd felt the difference and now she knew the cause. In the clinic she felt not only the genuine compassion of the doctors and nurses, but also the very real love of Christ...a love Keith had helped her find again.

A shadow still clung to her heart. "Help me, Lord," she said under her breath, "help me to trust you." Even as she prayed, she felt warmed by the memory of comforting broad shoulders and a slightly cynical smile. Kit straightened her shoulders. Uncle Edmund was a pathetic old man and she refused to give him the power to hurt her! Deliberately Kit turned her back on her hurtful memories. "What are you thinking about, Uncle?"

Picking up the hourglass, Edmund began turning it over in his hands. He stared at the streaming sand. "Look at the sand. I wonder if it understands its purpose, or does it just slide mindlessly from one end to the other?" His pale eyes watched the white stream of sand, but his face had a slack unfocused look. "At least the sand has a purpose, whether it knows it or not. For me, things get more vague all the time." Sighing, he clutched the hourglass.

Not knowing what to say, Kit watched the sand in the hourglass. Finally she asked, "What is *your* purpose, Uncle Edmund?"

The old man shrugged his thin shoulders in a movement more calculating than careless. "Happiness, wealth, what else is there?"

"Those are not my goals," said Kit softly.

Edmund stared at Kit in some bewilderment. "It's been mine. But not yet. I will have it. I will have it all." His intensity sent another shiver down Kit's spine.

"What is it you want, Uncle?"

Edmund watched the hourglass for a while before answering. His voice sounded distant. "They kept me from what I desired most, you know. Not my fault. *Ya*, they did it. Nothing I could do."

"What are you talking about, Uncle Edmund?"

"Clara and...Kat. Kat went off and left me. She went off like Clara and left me alone. She didn't care about me." His whine irritated Kit.

"Why didn't you come to America sooner? Surely you weren't helpless."

Edmund's head jerked up. His eyes glittering, he stared down at the hourglass clasped tightly in his blue-veined hands.

Not knowing exactly why, Kit shuddered. Yet, she forced a cheerful smile. "Gramma says you were quite the ladies' man when you were younger."

The old man grunted. "Didn't matter to Kat. She left me. She wouldn't listen. We could have had a good life, *ya*."

"I guess," said Kit, her voice soft. "Katalina didn't love you as much as you loved her." Silently she thanked God this pathetic old man was not her grandfather.

Sitting back, Edmund closed his eyes. The veins on his neck bulged blue against the chalky whiteness of his skin. A moment later his eyelids shot open and he glared with repugnance toward his son, who snored loudly on the sofa.

Sighing, Edmund again closed his eyes. But before he closed them he looked at Kit with such malice, she hugged her arms to her chest. When she would have risen, Edmund's voice stopped her.

"Kat loved me, but you know Katalina...always the butterfly. So pretty. So bright. And her smile. Why, it's for me! It is!" Edmund stared into space. After a pause, he growled, "Uncle Al again. Always in the way."

"Wasn't Katalina his niece?" Curiosity forced the question.

Edmund frowned and focused his gaze on her. "Kat, you can't spend all your time with your uncle. You have your own life to live. You belong to me. Let's go away now, today. Leave the old man. You'll do better on your own without him."

"Do better?" Kit asked. Despite her growing uneasiness, she felt the need to learn more about her namesake, her grandmother.

"Um, Kat." Edmund seemed to return to the present, but his gaze remained unfocused. "She played until you wanted to laugh, to weep. She wrote songs, too." His voice roughened. "But always, it was the old man first. His needs and his career. His career!"

Glaring at her, Edmund sniffed. "He was a hymn writer. Can you imagine Kat wasting herself doting on that old man? I tried. I tried to make her see what she was doing, but she wouldn't listen. She wouldn't leave that doddering old fool. So I helped." He laughed, a deep guttural laugh. "I dressed the old man. I put him to bed. He was like the dead, yet she wouldn't leave him."

Rubbing the goosebumps on her arms, Kit leaned away from Edmund's intense gaze. "What about—"

Edmund rambled on as though he hadn't heard her. "She said he was her uncle and she loved him. He was there for her when she needed him, she said, so she wanted to be there for him when he needed her. Nonsense."

Edmund lowered his voice and Kit realized he no longer knew she was beside him. "She would have come away with me in time. The fire, I thought she'd come after the fire. Not my fault. I didn't know the tree was so dry. I lit those candles to please her." He paused. "She screamed, and tried to put out the fire. She tried to save that worthless old man, but I wouldn't let her. I saved her. I saved *her*." He licked his lips. "No, you can't go back, Kat. Let him go. He only screamed once. Kat, don't leave me. Kat, I love you!"

"Dear Lord," Kit prayed. "He sounds like a raving lunatic. What do I do?" Afraid to stay, yet afraid to leave, Kit hugged her arms to her chest as she tried to ignore the fanatical light in Edmund's eerie gaze.

"You left me," he accused Kit. "You left me for a farmer. I hate your farmer! Your fault. All your fault. And Clara's. You shouldn't have come back, Kat. Better off dead, *ya*. You make trouble, as always. Make me remember."

Shivering, Kit watched him sag into the chair and stare at the hourglass that he once again began turning over and over. As panic overcame her, she jumped to her feet. She could feel hate emanating from him, reaching out menacingly, trying to envelop her in its monstrous grip. Hurriedly, she limped from the room.

In the bedroom she shut the door, shut out the monster. "Lord, there is something wrong in this place. It isn't Lars, after all. It's Uncle Edmund." She paced the bedroom floor. "He thinks I'm Katalina. I'm frightened. Lord what do I do?"

Kit rubbed her forehead. She seldom suffered headaches, but now her head throbbed. Why was she afraid of that pathetic shell of a man? Sitting on her bed, she closed her eyes to ease the pain. At least she had learned one important fact. She knew why her grandmother ran away. In his selfishness, Edmund had let a helpless old man burn to death.

Twisting the gold bracelet on her arm, Kit almost felt sorry for him. Everyone ran away from Edmund: Kat, Clara, even his wife. All he had left from his misspent life was Lars...and his hate.

He hated Gramma Clara, too. Why? Did he hate her for leaving him? But he came to America and they were reunited. It was obvious Clara loved her brother. Something didn't quite fit. Pieces of the puzzle remained missing. Maybe Uncle Edmund's mind was going. It was another frightening consideration.

Somehow, she was the catalyst that started a dangerous course of events she didn't comprehend. Perhaps her presence opened doors long dormant.

There were too many secrets. Resolutely lifting her chin, Kit determined, for her own peace of mind and the safety of her aunt, to do all she could to uncover the secrets her relatives tried so hard, for so long, to cover up. Those secrets unbalanced the minds of those who held them. They turned this home into a house haunted by tension and hatred.

If only Keith was here. Surely with his calm logic he would evaporate her fears. Unless there was no logic to the fierce emotions gripping those within the well cared for house. Sighing, Kit banished Keith's comforting visage from her mind. He was definitely her friend. *Was he more?* She shook her head to clear her thoughts, wishing Sally and her aunt would return.

Though reluctant to leave the security of the bedroom, Kit headed toward the kitchen for something to quench her thirst. She was relieved when she heard Sally at the backdoor.

"Please, dearie," called Sally, "could you hold the door? A little wider. There, that's good."

Augusta hobbled in on crutches, her ankle firmly bandaged. Once in the kitchen, she slumped into a chair and rubbed her arms. "Kit, how did you ever manage crutches after your surgery?"

"You get used them. After a while you won't be so sore."

"I don't know." Nervously fingering a crutch, Augusta shook her head, her hand. "How is Mother? Is she all right?"

Kit's insides twisted at the thought she might have failed her grandmother. "I don't know. She hasn't called out or anything."

"I'm sure she's simply sleeping," Sally soothed them both. "I'll check." With that, Sally left them to check on Clara. But she soon reappeared. "Clara's fine, Augusta, sound asleep just as I left her. Stop worrying about your mother. It's you who needs a nurse now."

Augusta grimaced. "What am I to do? There's so much to do around here. How can I do it all with a sprained ankle?"

"It *is* just a sprain?" Kit asked.

"*Ya*, I really should get up and start lunch."

"Pooh." Sally opened the refrigerator. "Now you just relax. I'll fix sandwiches and a salad. Usually you're at work and I do this anyway, so calm down."

Augusta protested, "I should help."

"No," Kit echoed Sally's command.

"Maybe I'll dust then."

"You'll stay right there, Augusta," Sally said firmly. "When it needs doing, I'll see to it."

Sally's ability to command Augusta surprised Kit. Maybe that explained their long friendship. Augusta needed someone strong like Sally to lean on. Thoughtfully, Kit helped Sally fix the small but tasteful lunch.

When she called the two men to the table, both seemed in unusually good humor. Edmund seemed more alert than Kit had ever seen him. Gone was the hateful old man she had encountered earlier. Even Lars was not overly obnoxious until he pulled out his usual after meal cigar. Augusta protested until Edmund scowled and ordered him to take it outside. Lars merely rolled his eyes.

Kit breathed a thankful prayer that this was not her home. How much better the love she sensed in Keith's sister's home. How long had Gramma put up with this? Or were things different before she grew ill?

Feeling restless, Kit returned to her bedroom. Even without the tangible hate Edmund manifested earlier, the house had a tense, waiting feeling that made her edgy. The feeling grew stronger as she entered the bedroom door. Her suitcase stuck out from the behind the bed oddly. Kit gulped. Someone had moved it. With shaking hands, Kit hauled the case on the bed and opened it.

Her mouth dropped open. There, nestled snugly in the bottom of the case, sat her jewelry box. Gingerly picking it up, she opened it. The few pieces of jewelry she kept inside were still there, but, as they weren't all that valuable, this didn't surprise her. Her gnarled fingers caressed the polished surface of the box. Not a scratch marred its smooth surface.

Clutching the box, Kit frowned. Though relieved to have it back, the question remained. Who had taken it? Who had returned it and why? Here was another puzzle piece that didn't quite fit. Somehow this innocent looking box played a part in the frightening drama unfolding around her.

Hearing Augusta's clumping crutches, she hastily returned the box to the suitcase. By the time her aunt entered the room, Kit sat on the bed reading her Bible.

Keith Long shifted uncomfortably on the cushioned chair that creaked a warning. Extreme boredom threatened to overtake him as the speaker droned on.

His attention wandered from the speaker, and Kit's image filled his mind. His lips quirked as he recalled the softness of her skin, the laughter in her large eyes, and the way she fit so naturally in his arms. He felt the urge to call her, but couldn't just get up and leave.

His smile faded and he was gripped with the certainty Kit needed him. He shook his head. A rational man, he wasn't given to such fantasies. Still, he reminded himself, prayer never hurt. Though his eyes focused on the speaker, Keith lifted Kit and her situation to the one whom they both served.

CHAPTER TEN

They encourage themselves in a matter: they commune of laying snares privily; they say, Who shall see them? Psalm 64:5

Leaning heavily on her crutches, Augusta clumped awkwardly into the bedroom. With an obvious sigh of relief, her aunt leaned the crutches against the wall before sitting on the bed.

"Anything I can do for you?" asked Kit.

Augusta shook her head. "*Nej tack*, Kit. No, thank you."

"Want me to leave you so you can rest?"

"I don't know. I don't much feel like sleeping." Her expression sent a desperate plea for Kit to stay.

On the bed opposite, Kit closed her Bible and set it on the nightstand. She would have liked to ask her aunt about the jewelry box, but she'd promised Gramma Clara not to discuss it. Not with anyone. Maybe, she could approach the subject another way.

"Have you notice anything missing around here lately?" she asked offhandedly.

Too obvious, she thought.

Augusta hesitated. "Why...I haven't lost anything, have you?"

Kit noticed her aunt didn't meet her eyes. Thoughtfully she studied the other woman's face. "You didn't decide to help me out by emptying out my suitcase, did you, Aunt Augusta?" Although she chose her words with care, even to her own ears, her question sounded like an accusation. Her aunt's anger didn't surprise her.

Augusta flushed. "Is there any reason why I'd want to go through your suitcase? What are you suggesting, Kit?"

Kit sighed. "It's nothing, Aunt Augusta. I'm sorry. I just mislaid something and wondered if you'd seen it."

Augusta visibly relaxed. Reaching down, she pulled off her shoes and lay back on the bed with a sigh. "I guess I am tired after all," she murmured with a weak smile in Kit's direction. Closing her eyes, she turned away from Kit. A few minutes later her breathing slowed rhythmically. Waiting a minute longer to be sure her aunt was asleep, Kit pushed herself to her feet and tiptoed from the room.

Feeling cramped in the small house, Kit shifted from room to room. Though it was larger than her own apartment in Kearney, somehow here she felt cramped and uneasy. She missed the informality, and the easy pace of her mid-western town.

She missed her friends. She missed...Taking a deep breath, Kit faced her thoughts squarely. She missed Dr. Keith Long. If only she felt free to call him. Would he think she was chasing him? Faint color rose in her cheeks. That would never do! He must never know how he affected her.

Absently, she checked her watch. Besides, he would be at his convention and she could hardly disturb him there. Nevertheless, she checked her handbag. Carrying it to the dining room, she rifled through her wallet to make sure she still had the card with his phone number on it.

For a moment she panicked, thinking she'd lost it. No, there it was. The intensity of her relief unsettled her. Holding the card in her hand, she realized it had only his sister's number on it. She couldn't call him now, anyway. Still, just thinking about him made her feel better. Later, if she gathered the courage, she'd call.

Picking up a magazine from the sideboard, Kit sat down to read. Leafing through the pages, she spotted an article that looked interesting. At that moment she heard Augusta moan. Throwing down the magazine, Kit rushed to the bedroom to her aunt's side. Augusta lay curled on the bed, her hair disheveled and her sweaty hands tight against her face.

"Aunt Augusta, what's wrong? What happened?"

"Oh, I don't know." Raising her head, she stared at her niece. "A nightmare. It was a horrible nightmare." Reaching out, she clutched Kit's arm. "What am I to do? I'm scared!"

Kit sat down on the edge of Augusta's bed. "What frightened you? Another dream?"

Her aunt nodded. "My nightmares. They're back again, just like before." She covered her face before glancing at Kit. "I'm afraid...afraid of losing my mind. Why are they coming back? What am I going to do?"

Augusta's terror rippled through Kit, who grasped her hand to calm her down. "Aunt Augusta, is it really so bad? Why don't you tell me about your nightmare? Maybe that will help. We'll fight it together."

"I can't! I can't! It was too awful." She stared at Kit through wild eyes. "I mustn't think about it. They told me not to think about it."

At that moment Sally marched into the room. Her cheerful countenance sobered at the sight of Augusta's distress. "What's wrong, Augusta?"

Kit answered, "Auntie had another nightmare. I figured talking about it might help."

"Oh, no. It's too awful." Augusta's trembling fingers picked at the bed covers.

"Why not, Augusta?" coaxed Sally, plunking down next to Kit on edge of Augusta's bed. "Everyone has nightmares, Augusta. Tell us about it." Her weight tilted the bed toward the floor and Kit had to brace her feet to keep from sliding off. "Come now, tell us about it." Kit heard the note of command.

Apparently Augusta heard it as well. She closed her eyes and swallowed hard. Her voice hushed and hesitant, she said, "I was at home with Mother and Father. It was all so strange, because Uncle Edmund was also there." She glanced from Kit to Sally. "That can't be, can it?"

"It was only a dream," Kit soothed. "Anyone can be in a dream."

"I guess so." Augusta sounded unconvinced.

"What happened?" Sally coached.

"Uncle Edmund, all smiles, came. He and Father played some kind of game. As they played they both got louder and louder and louder." Augusta covered her ears. "Uncle Edmund jumped up. Father sank down. Uncle Edmund ran away. I screamed at him to come back. He pushed me. I fell down beside Father...all in little pieces. That's when I woke up."

"Does this mean anything to you, Augusta?" asked Sally, surveying her friend through narrowed eyes.

"I don't know. I don't understand." There was a childish plea in her voice.

"Well," said Kit firmly, "maybe it was a nightmare and nothing else. It's over. Right, Sally?"

Glancing at the nurse for support, she noted anxiety in her eyes. The nurse reached for one of the bottles beside the bed. "Kit, please get me some water."

Together they made Augusta comfortable once more. They left her drowsy from the pill Sally gave her. Kit followed Sally to the kitchen. At Sally's invitation, she settled down on a chair to share afternoon tea. As the nurse brought the tea to the table, Kit voiced her concern.

"You don't really believe Augusta's dream was so innocent, do you?"

Gingerly, Sally sat down on the chair that creaked under her bulk. "Aye, dearie, her nightmares do concern me." She paused as though searching for words to express her concern. "We know Claus died of a heart condition. He died because Augusta didn't bring him his pills fast enough. Naturally, Augusta blamed herself. She literally 'went to pieces.'"

Kit sat up. "Like her dream."

"Aye, like the dream. Subconsciously, she hasn't ever gotten over her part in her father's death."

Kit mulled the information, but it didn't quite fit what Gramma Clara told her. "Gramma was there. Right there, I mean."

"She was there, but she wouldn't ever talk about it afterward. I suppose she wanted to protect her only daughter. Augusta hasn't been too stable since then. All it'll take is some big upset, and...." Sally shrugged.

"So that's the reason everyone's afraid to talk about what happened, afraid of how it will affect Aunt Augusta."

"Reasonable enough, isn't it?" Sally sipped her tea.

"But, if Augusta caused the death of her father, and the dream certainly seems to indicate it is about his death, then what was Uncle Edmund doing in the picture?"

Sally frowned. Her pudgy hands gripped the fragile cup. "I don't know, dearie." She added cautiously, "That bothers me as well."

"Could Uncle Edmund have been there as well?"

"Hardly." Sally laughed, but Kit noticed her wide mouth was tight. "You forget. Edmund came over a year later...after Claus died."

Kit drank her tea slowly. "Oh, I see."

Cocking her ear, Sally set down her cup. "Oh dear, I think I hear Clara." She heaved her bulk up from the chair. "I'd better go check."

"I'll wash up these dishes," Kit called after her. After running water, Kit carried the cups to the sink. Her thoughts whirled in confusion.

Augusta lay in a drugged sleep, and Kit knew why. Her aunt feared for her sanity because of recurring nightmares that hadn't plagued her in years. Why was she having the dreams? Why had they started up again after all this time? Was the fault hers? *Oh, Lord, no.* But it had to be. Augusta didn't start having them again until just after Kit arrived.

Something was wrong. The pieces didn't fit. What was she missing? And where did Edmund fit into this distorted picture? Suddenly she recalled the picture of Edmund in the photo album. As soon as she wiped the cups and saucers, Kit went to find the albums. They weren't easy to find. She remembered placing them in Gramma Clara's room, but for some reason she found them on the sideboard.

Opening the albums, Kit flipped through them until she found the picture of Augusta beside a handsome blond dandy with a careless smile. Lars said the young man was Uncle Edmund. Bending closer, Kit examined the photograph. With a trembling finger she traced Edmund's long, blond mustache.

It was the mustache that caught Kit's attention. Could it be that Edmund played a part not only in her aunt's latest nightmare, but in the previous one as well? She considered Augusta's first nightmare. Could the cold, slimy, yellow hair thing possibly be...a mustache?

Kit shook her head. Did she truly think she'd be able to solve the mystery behind her aunt's horrifying nightmares in such a short time? At any rate she mustn't mention her suspicions to Augusta, or anyone else in the house for that matter. Still, if Edmund *had* been a part of those nightmares, could he also have been a part of the real incident?

That would mean Edmund had to have been in the country long before he, and everyone else, claimed. Or, hadn't they known? The implications made Kit's stomach churn. Unfortunately this wasn't a mystery book she could lay aside when things became too intense. She was living the mystery, and didn't like the tangible taste of fear it left in her mouth. This was real, all too real.

However much she wanted to find a place to feel secure, her aunt was asleep in the bedroom and she didn't want to disturb her. As much as she wished the frightening predicament in which she now found herself would go away, she knew withdrawing wasn't the answer. Instead, she must push forward. Only the truth would set her, and her aunt, free. The thought brought a smile. How many times had Dr. Ellis and her physical therapist coaxed, encouraged, and even raged at her as she timidly relearned how to walk?

"Step out. Step forward."

"Don't be afraid, I'm here to catch you if you fall."

"Step forward in faith. You can do it. Trust me."

Only now the words sounded inside her, and they didn't come from any human source. *"Trust me."*

After surgery the doctor had cheered her on as she timidly tottered forward first on full-length leg braces and crutches, then on two crutches, one, then none. The doctor's confidence provided her with the confidence she needed to keep trying. It was those long months of surgery and recovery that turned a doctor-patient relationship into one of profound respect and enduring friendship.

"Trust me."

Keith, too, echoed those words. Kit did trust him. Just thinking about him made her palms sweaty and her heart increase its pace. She desired his presence with a desperation that shocked her. How she needed the comfort and strength of his arms holding her tight. How she longed to listen to his deep, calming voice dispelling her fears.

"What absolute nonsense," she scolded herself furiously. "Stop this! Get a grip."

But even her wayward thoughts didn't keep at bay the sense that some terrifying force ruled this house. The force whirled around her, sucking her into its vortex.

"If only Keith were here now," she murmured.

"I'm here! Trust me!" The words in her mind were no longer a whisper.

"God loves you. He has taken care of you," Keith had said.

Bowing her head, Kit clasped her hands. *Lord, I feel very alone. I'm afraid. I don't know what to do. Help me to trust you. Give me courage and wisdom. Amen.*

A stillness settled gently over her frightened heart. "I will trust you, Lord, I will!" When Kit lifted her head, her chin raised with determination. She recalled the stubbornness she'd needed to walk again; she'd be just as resolved now.

As though guided, Kit walked into the living room and sat down beside Uncle Edmund. "Would you tell me about your first impressions of America?" she asked.

Straightening his shoulders, Edmund turned the hourglass over again. *For at least the millionth time*, thought Kit. A slight smile played at the corners of his drawn lips.

"Sweden was home no longer to me. Kat was gone and Clara was in America. So I came over, too."

"You married?"

"Clara wanted me to settle down. So I married to please her."

Kit struggled to keep her repugnance to herself. "You got married just to please your sister?"

"It didn't though. She didn't like Lizzy. Never could please my saintly sister. Always she sided against me."

"I understand Gramma Clara tried to protect you from your own destructive behavior."

"Well, you understand wrong. I wasn't such a bad lad. High spirited, *ya*. She shouldn't have sided with Kat against me. Shouldn't have taken what belongs to me." Edmund's eyes glittered, and his teeth rasped together.

"Gramma would never take what didn't belong to her," Kit protested.

"Think not?" The old man laughed derisively. "Maybe you don't know your grandmother as well as you think you do. I know what you came for, and you won't get it!" Waving a fist in her face, he all but shouted, "You hear? You won't get it!"

Kit shot to her feet. "I came because Gramma asked for me. You keep her estate. I, for one, wish Gramma would live forever. Even if you don't." Oh dear, what had she just implied?

"You think I wish her to die, is that it?" Edmund's glittering eyes narrowed. "What chance do I have then of getting back my own?"

Wondering what he referred to, Kit frowned at him. "What does she have of yours that is so important?"

Edmund glanced away. "Nothing. Nothing that should matter to you. Clara has it. It belongs, rightfully, to me."

Kit thought of the jewelry box and Gramma Clara's concern that it be passed on to its rightful owner. "If it's yours, why hasn't she returned it then?"

At this, the old man shrank back into the chair mumbling, "What do a couple of pieces of paper matter to her?"

Kit shifted her weight. "So why are they so important to you? What are they?" When Edmund didn't respond, Kit repeated the question.

His gaze distant, Edmund smiled slyly. Kit got the impression he relived the past. "I suppose you helped Claus with the farm when you first arrived?"

Edmund shot forward in his chair. Even Lars put down the paper to stare at him. "I didn't! Of course I didn't! He stole Kat, and my sister away from me. Help him? Why I—" He slumped. "How could I help Claus?" he whined. "He was already long buried by the time I arrived."

"I guess I still haven't gotten the family's history properly worked out in my mind." Kit shrugged. "Maybe you can help me sort it out." Kit waited, but the old man was either ignoring her or was once more reliving the past. She again felt hate emanating from him, felt panic rise up inside her.

"You'll get nothing further from him now," Lars snorted. "He doesn't even know you exist." With that he returned to his reading as though he, too, would wipe out her existence.

As Kit left the room she couldn't help the feeling that Uncle Edmund had almost made some disastrous slip. Could it be he *was* in America before Claus died? *It's high time I talk to Gramma Clara again.*

Back in the bedroom she found Augusta trying to position her crutches comfortably under her sore arms. "Try to put more of your weight on your hands where you grip the crutch, rather than all under your arms," Kit advised her.

Augusta adjusted the crutches once more and clumped forward. "It does help. *Tack så mycket.* Thank you very much, Kit."

Still, her aunt swayed dangerously as she made her way slowly to the bathroom. Biting her lip, Kit prayed she'd keep her balance. She sighed in relief as her aunt reached the safety of the bathroom. But as she turned away, a crash spun her around so fast she almost fell. "Sally! Sally!" screamed Kit. "It's Augusta!"

Lars sauntered in from the living room and stared at his aunt as though she were a freak in a circus show. "Lars, help!" cried Kit, reaching for her aunt. Frustrated, she grabbed the doorframe to keep from falling over her aunt.

As usual, it was Sally who helped Augusta to her feet. "Lars, get those crutches," ordered Sally.

Reluctantly, Lars picked them up and ungraciously handed them to his cousin. With a feral smile on his thick lips, he watched as Sally helped Augusta, pale and shaken, back to the bedroom. Turning on his heel, Lars walked briskly back to the living room.

Clenching her fists at her side, Kit stilled the rage simmering inside as she turned back to the bathroom doorway. There was something strange about the way her aunt fell, as though catapulted forward. When Kit first used crutches she remembered falling, but it wasn't anything like the way her aunt fell.

Stepping toward the door, she surveyed the opening. *Oh, no!* Her hand at her throat, she stared in disbelief at the nearly invisible cord strung across the threshold...just high enough for someone to catch their toe. A deliberately set trap.

One thing was certain, Augusta had once again suffered a manufactured "accident." Who was the intended victim? What would happen next?

Somehow Lars had a part in this, of this Kit was sure. Well, almost sure.

This time, she *knew* she needed someone's help and advice. This time she knew she had to reach Keith.

CHAPTER ELEVEN

This is the dream; and we will tell the interpretation thereof before the king. Daniel 2:36.

A weak summons interrupted Kit's contemplation. Gramma! Tiptoeing into her grandmother's bedroom, she thought Gramma Clara appeared weaker. Maybe it was the fragile transparency of her skin, or the slight diffusion of her gaze. "What can I do for you, Gramma?" Kit leaned close.

"Noise. What happened?" Gramma Clara's voice came out in a whisper.

Of all times to hear the commotion. "Aunt Augusta fell." Kit bit her lip. "Don't worry, Gramma, Sally's taking care of her. She'll be fine. It shook her up, I'm sure, but she's fine." Kit couldn't bring herself to tell her grandmother what she'd discovered.

"Again?" Gramma frowned. "Odd she should fall twice in so many days."

"You knew!"

Clara nodded. Her parchment-like fingers grasped Kit's hand.

"*Var snäll och var försiktig.* Please be careful." The old woman's hand dropped limply onto the bedcovers. Her eyes closed.

Straightening, Kit turned to leave. "Wait!" whispered Clara. Kit swung back.

"I'm here, Gramma."

"You're certain Augusta is all right?" Worry lit her eyes.

Kit patted her grandmother's hand. Beneath her light touch, it felt so fragile. "She was dazed and confused, but otherwise seemed all right."

"Did she have...another nightmare?"

Kit nodded. "Yes. How did you know?"

Gramma Clara turned her head, but not before Kit witnessed the fear in her faded eyes.

Kit tightened her grip on her Grandmother's hand. "Gramma, what's wrong? Please tell me."

Tears shimmered in the old woman's eyes. "Help her, Kit. Don't let her remember. For all our sakes, don't let her remember. It may..." Her grandmother's words trailed off and Kit leaned close to catch the last. Even then she was not certain she had heard the strange word correctly. *"Varning."*

The ominous sounding word pursued Kit as she left her grandmother's room. Needing a quiet place to think, she sought the solace of the hot, muggy, closet of a back porch. Outside the small window, the scorched lawn simmered under the burning sun. A few strong flowers braved the blistering heat, but most were slowly shriveling, and dying...just like Gramma Clara.

Varning. What did it mean? It sounded like *warning*. Why hadn't Kit applied herself when she had the opportunity to learn the tongue of her ancestors?

Overhead, a few robins swayed back and forth on the high telephone wires. When a gust of wind hit the wire, they fluttered and flew away as one. Just as suddenly Kit gasped. All this time she had seen her aunt as Gramma Clara's protector. What if Kit had it all backwards?

Was Gramma, instead, the protector? Did Augusta hold inside her mind some secret so devastating someone would seek to do her harm rather than have the secret revealed? Had Gramma Clara protected her daughter the only way she knew how, by imposing the years of silence and secrecy?

"Oh, Lord!" Kit floundered helplessly. "Am I to blame for Augusta's injuries? Is someone trying to harm her because I'm helping her remember? Lord, I'm not worth it. Maybe I was right." All her fears and doubts about both herself and God's love, enveloped her.

"Trust me!" The voice inside her head startled Kit. *"Trust me!"*

Kit gulped as tears filled her eyes. "Help me, Lord. Help me to trust you. It's so hard."

"Trust me!"

Kit bowed her head. "I will. *I will!*"

It was too late to pretend dangerous memories had not surfaced. There was no time to muck about in self-pity. Somehow, some way Kit knew she had to find the answer. Gramma Clara couldn't protect her daughter any longer. Only by exposing the long held secret would her aunt be free and, hopefully, safe.

Kit focused her thoughts on the problem at hand. Who knew this secret? Gramma Clara surely knew. Uncle Edmund possibly knew as well, but he wasn't up to setting those traps. Lars wasn't old enough...unless he'd found out somehow. But how could it affect him? Kit shook her head. It was all so confusing.

Far away in the dining room, Kit heard the phone and slowly went to answer it. Her breath caught at the sound of Keith's deep voice. "How you doing?"

"Oh, Keith." Kit couldn't hide her relief. "I'm so glad you called. I was thinking of calling you later on."

"You know what they say about great minds." Keith chuckled.

"Right." Kit forced herself to remain calm. "How's the conference?" She glanced toward the living room, where Edmund stared at the hourglass and Lars snored softly.

"Rather boring, actually," Keith admitted. "I'd like to see you again, Kit."

Warmth curled around Kit's heart and she found it hard to breathe. "I'd like to see you again, too," she managed to squeak.

"How about that date to ValleyFair? You will go with me, won't you?"

Kit's wobbly knees refused to support her and she sank down on the straight-backed chair by the phone. "Date!" Surely he was only teasing, she reminded herself sharply. "When?" She squeezed her eyes closed.

"Are you all right?" he snapped. As soon as Keith spoke, she knew her hesitation and trembling voice transmitted her anxiety through to him. "Has something happened? If something's wrong, I want to know."

Desperately Kit wished to share her fears and suspicions with Keith and glean some of his wisdom. But this was neither the proper time nor place. "I'm all right. It's Aunt Augusta. She sprained her ankle. She fell with her crutches. There's something else, but I can't talk about it now." Kit clutched the phone, and prayed silently that Keith wouldn't hang up. Not yet. "When will I see you?"

"Will tomorrow afternoon be too late? I thought we'd go then."

Way too late, she cried silently. *I need you now!*

Out loud she said, "Fine." Did she sound as forlorn as she felt?

"Kit," Keith said gently. "I'm sorry I can't stay on the phone longer, but I have to go. I'm on a pay phone, and..."

"Yes, yes, of course." Kit tried to keep her disappointment from her tone. "Thank you for calling."

"Kit." Keith hesitated. "If you really need me...."

Did he really want the truth? Kit shook her head. "Tomorrow will be fine."

"I'll be praying for you, Kit." The tenderness in his voice brought tears to her eyes.

"I need it." Kit wrapped the cord around her hand.

"Tomorrow then."

"Tomorrow," Kit echoed dismally. Hanging up the phone, Kit choked back the lump in her throat. For the space of the call, she'd felt safe and secure. Now the uneasy tension wrapped itself around her in its ever-tightening stranglehold.

When Lars snorted as she hung up, Kit sent up a silent "Thank you" that she hadn't confided in Keith over the phone. Turning heel, she went to check on her aunt. Augusta's still white form and glassy eyes frightened her. "Aunt Augusta, are you all right?"

Sally, still in the room, put a finger to her lips. "Dearie, all of this is too much for her," she whispered. "I'm afraid she's headed for another breakdown. I gave her something to calm her down."

Kit frowned as the nurse left to fix dinner. She didn't like having her aunt dependent upon the potent pills supplied by Sally, but what could she do about it?

With a sigh, Kit changed into her blue gown and brushed her hair before following the nurse to the kitchen to help prepare dinner. "Will Aunt Augusta be all right?"

"No way of knowing that, dearie." Sally turned from the stove. "It would be a shame to have to put her away again. Next time, without Clara, I doubt she'd ever get out."

"She has to get better." Kit twisted the gold bracelet on her arm.

"You're forgetting she is far from stable." A hiss of steam sounded as water dropped onto the burner.

"She'd be fine if someone wasn't so busy manufacturing "accidents" for her," retorted Kit.

Hands on her hips, Sally swung her bulk around to face Kit. "What are you saying?"

"Aunt Augusta didn't just fall this time anymore than she did the first time."

"What do you mean by that?" Sally's eyes narrowed.

"Someone strung a cord across the threshold. That's why she tripped."

Sally stiffened. "Come now, dearie."

"I'll show you. I saw the cord." Kit marched, or as much of a march as she could manage, to the bathroom.

Sally followed. "Cord? There's no cord here."

"It was *right* here." Kit's voice wavered.

With a sympathetic smile on her broad face, the nurse patted her shoulder like she was a dim-witted child. "There, there, dearie. It's all right."

Clenching her teeth, Kit moved away from the nurse's hand. "I did see it!"

"Sure you did, dearie," she soothed. "Why not lay down for awhile before dinner."

Kit ground her teeth, but said nothing. Frustrated, she limped into the bedroom and sank down on her bed. Thankfully Augusta, breathing slowly and deeply, had her face to the wall. "Lord, please help Aunt Augusta be all right," she whispered. "Me, too. Keep us safe through this night."

Tomorrow afternoon seemed an eternity away. Would Keith believe her story about the trap? Sally didn't. The cord *had* been more than her imagination! Kit knew what she'd seen. But someone had removed it.

Maybe the object was not so much to injure Augusta, as to drive her over the edge. Was someone so greedy for Gramma's estate they'd seek to harm Augusta?

And what about her? Both Uncle Edmund and Lars believed she had come to claim her part of the estate. Surely they didn't think to drive her crazy with childish pranks. But, she reminded herself, that loose step, while injuring and frightening Augusta, could have killed her. She shivered.

If she continued to insist she saw things no one else acknowledged seeing, would she, herself, not be effectively discredited? Hugging her arms to her chest, Kit whispered, "Keith I need you. We're in the hands of a fiend and I don't know what to do." She winced at how much she was beginning to sound like her indecisive aunt.

If only she could convince Sally. No, Sally was so used to dealing with sick people, she naturally assumed illness. There was no next move. There was only Keith, tomorrow...and only God now. She closed her eyes.

The faceless fiend knew the game; she did not. But God knew. *"Trust me,"* He said. Prayerfully, she opened her Bible.

Soaking up Proverbs like a sponge, Kit read for a long time in order to banish the doubts which lingered in her mind. As she closed the book, the verses from Proverbs 3:5 and 6 stayed in her mind. *"Trust in the Lord with all thine heart; and lean not unto thine own understanding. In all thy ways acknowledge him, and he shall direct thy paths."*

It wasn't easy to trust. Why was it easier to trust Keith whom she met just a few days ago, than to trust her Heavenly Father who had taken care of her all these years? Kit's thoughts drifted. Closing her eyes, she slept.

Keith stood beside her, holding her hand. "I love you Kit. Trust God. Trust me."

In her sleep, Kit smiled and murmured, *"Trust..."*

When Sally called them for dinner, she awoke refreshed. Even though she tried to lightly pass off her dream, bubbles of joy danced inside her.

Augusta, already awake, had just finished arranging her hair. Though her eyes had lost that glazed look, she still seemed slightly bewildered. Straightening her dress, her aunt slipped into her low heels.

"How are you feeling, Auntie?" Kit grabbed for her hairbrush.

"Much better, thank you." Reaching for her crutches, Augusta gingerly placed them under her arms.

Thoughtfully Kit watched her aunt. Should she tell her about the cord? If her aunt could tell her why someone might want to harm her, maybe it would help. But if she couldn't, telling her aunt might needlessly frighten her.

Instead, she wanted to try to get her aunt to remember. But was it worth the risk to Augusta's sanity? Was she not riding the edge even without that knowledge? Still, hadn't God promised that truth would set people free?

"Aunt Augusta, what do you remember about the night your father died?"

Augusta tensed. "No. NO! It's all so hazy."

"Do you think you might remember if you really tried?" Kit pulled a wide white belt about her waist, and slid her feet into a pair of white slippers.

"Maybe." Her aunt shook her head. "I...I've not tried. They said I mustn't."

"Forget them," coaxed Kit. "Do you recall your father's heart attack?"

Trembling, Augusta slumped onto the bed. "My...my fault. He got sweaty, weak, and begged me to get his pills. I was always so proud to help him." She tugged nervously at her skirt.

"So you brought them?"

"I...I think so." Perspiration beaded on Augusta's upper lip as her face contorted with suffering.

"You gave them to him," Kit encouraged her aunt.

Though her aunt shook, she didn't appear to be losing control. Maybe Augusta was stronger than anyone realized. Maybe she had never been able to put the incident behind her because no one would let her talk about it. What an awful thing to fester in one's mind. Kit understood. Had she not recently let go of her own hurt?

Kit prayed no one would interrupt them. "Ye-Yes. No. I...I was too...too late." Her face pale, she stared at Kit. "You understand. I was too late." Augusta closed her eyes.

"Were you and Gramma the only ones with your father that night?"

"Yes." Suddenly Augusta's eyes flew open.

Kit leaned forward. "What is it, Aunt Augusta? What do you remember?" She reached a hand out for her aunt, but Augusta pushed it away.

"N...nothing. I remember nothing." Terror stared from her tight face.

"It's all right, Augusta. There's no one here but you and me. And I won't hurt you." What had her aunt remembered that so terrified her?

"Hey, you two. Didn't you hear me call you to dinner?"

"We'll be right out, Sally," Kit called.

Augusta clumped out on her crutches as though fearing Kit might try to restrain her with questions. Kit couldn't hide her grin. It seemed her aunt was, after all, getting the hang of walking on crutches. Following her aunt, Kit kept an eye out for any more "traps."

They joined the others already seated at the table. As she ate, Kit surreptitiously surveyed the others. Uncle Edmund kept his head down. Lars smirked as he caught her eye. Augusta answered in hesitant monosyllables whenever Sally spoke to her. Kit sensed an eerie stillness, like the calm just before a tornado hurls down from the sky, destroying everything in its path.

After dinner, Kit ensconced herself in the bedroom. She had been relieved when Lars and his father left directly after dinner, mumbling something about car repairs. Kit only felt relief. She left Sally and her aunt conversing, munching eclairs, and sipping coffee and tea at the table.

Alone in the bedroom, Kit swung her suitcase onto the bed and snapped it open. Good, the jewelry box was still safe. Sitting down on the bed, she held the box in her lap and carefully caressed its smooth surface. Somehow this innocent little box played a part in the strange drama whirling about her in this house. *How?* There must be a clue. Kit wished she had some idea of what she was looking for.

Why had Gramma Clara asked her to bring the box to the city, if she didn't even want to see it? And why did her grandmother make her promise not to reveal its presence to anyone else? Someone did know, because someone took the box and then returned it. What connection, if any, did it have to her aunt's "accidents"?

Sighing, Kit opened the lid. As long as it had been in the family, someone surely would have discovered any secrets it might contain. Was that it? Or perhaps the secret no longer existed, and someone was angry.

Frowning, Kit gingerly probed the velvety interior of the box. Carefully she prodded, stretched, and patted the worn lining. She could almost feel her namesake, Katalina, calling to her from the dim past. Of course that was silly. Still, she had a very real sense of being directed. She smiled at her vivid imagination.

About ready to give up, Kit felt her spirits lift when she uncovered a small screw in one corner of the box. No other corner had one. She found a nail file and applied it to the screw. It refused to budge. Gritting her teeth, she used both hands. Ever so slightly, it gave. Up popped a tiny handle. Kit pulled. The whole velvet-covered bottom ended up in her hand. The jewelry box had a false bottom and the compartment, though quite small, held a prize.

Hands shaking with excitement, Kit carefully pulled out four folded pieces of parchment-like paper. Gently she unfolded them, fearing they might disintegrate in her hands. It was hand-printed sheet music! Four songs by...Kit squinted to read the faded ink.

"Oh, my," she gasped. "A. L. Augustafson."

Trying to still her trembling hands, she refolded the music and hid it once more in the jewelry box. Furtively glancing toward the door, she hurriedly, but carefully, tightened the screw. Her thoughts racing, Kit put the box back in her suitcase. Who had put the music sheets in the box?

A. L. Augustafson had been a legend even while he lived. Kit's mother told her about him. He'd been a famous songwriter, but became even more so after becoming a Christian. Any manuscript of his would have been valuable even back then, but now the implications staggered Kit.

Questions remained. Who put the music sheets in the box? Who knew about them? Is this why Gramma Clara asked her to bring the jewelry box? Why now? Had someone found out about them...someone who had no right to them?

If only she had a better place to hide them. But, if someone else had already discovered the manuscripts, why hadn't they taken them? She must ask Gramma to explain. This whole mystery had gone on far too long. Things were getting out of hand and she desperately needed advice.

While things didn't add up, there was nothing more she could do today. Tomorrow she'd ask Gramma Clara to explain. Tomorrow she would be with Keith.

CHAPTER TWELVE

And they shall say unto them, Hear, 0 Israel, ye approach this day unto battle against your enemies: let not your hearts faint not, and do not tremble, either be ye terrified because of them. Deuteronomy 20:3

Kit awoke early. She felt scarcely less exhausted than when she went to bed. Her gown clung to her oppressively. Breathing the hot stuffy air, she fervently wished her grandmother had air conditioning. Since she'd been here, despite the heat, not even the window cooler in the living room had been turned on.

Sitting up, she pulled open the curtains at the head of her bed. Sunlight poured into the room, over both her bed and Augusta's, lighting her aunt's slack face. Augusta's arm hung limply from the sheet. For once she hadn't been plagued with nightmares. Sally's pills must have laid her out pretty good. Maybe too good. Frowning, Kit leaned forward for a closer look. Her aunt seemed almost too relaxed.

Still frowning, Kit swung to her feet and grabbed up a pair of navy slacks and a white cotton shirt then went to the bathroom to shower and to dress.

Half an hour later as she brushed out her wet hair, Kit glanced up from the bathroom mirror to the small round blue and yellow clock on the shelf. Good! Sally would soon be arriving and she could ask her to check on Augusta.

After the nurse got Gramma up and ready for the day, Kit had every intention of seeing her grandmother. Time was running out. This time she must get her to explain about the jewelry box.

She almost persuaded herself to talk to her grandmother before Sally arrived, but thought better of it. Instead she took her things back to the bedroom. Augusta swaying, confused and still groggy from her drugged sleep, belted her robe about her. Tucking her crutches under her arms, she said, "I must check on Mother. Should have been up an hour ago. I can't imagine how I could have slept so long? Oh, dear."

Sitting down suddenly, Augusta rubbed her forehead. "Has Sally arrived, yet? I feel woozy."

"Gramma's probably still asleep. I've heard nothing from her, and I've been up for some time. I'm sure Sally will be here any minute. Don't worry, I'll stay with you until she gets here." Kit reached for her aunt, who shook her head.

"No, go on." She got up. "See, I'm better all ready. I'll be out as soon as I dress.

Still, Kit hesitated. "If you're sure." When her aunt motioned for her to, she said, "I'll find us something to eat."

"Just for yourself, please, Kit. I'll get something later. *Tack så mycket.*"

"Fine. If you're sure you're all right?" At her aunt's nod, Kit slipped from the room, and left her aunt to dress in privacy. In the kitchen she fixed herself a peanut butter and honey sandwich on whole wheat bread, poured herself a tall glass of milk and sat down to her usual breakfast.

The back door opened. "Morning, dearie," Sally called from the porch. "How's everything this morning?"

"Oh, hi, Sally. Guess what? Aunt Augusta didn't have any nightmares last night. She did seem a little dizzy this morning, though. Maybe you should check on her."

Sally frowned. "She didn't fall, did she?"

"No."

"Good. She's probably just woozy from the medicine she took." The nurse rumbled into the room and lay her bulging purse on the kitchen table. "And your grandmother?"

"Still sleeping, I guess. I didn't think I should wake her."

"You did the right thing, Kit. Guess I'd better get right in there."

"You'll check on Auntie as well?"

Sally nodded. "I'll do that." Glancing toward Kit, she said, "I didn't see Lars' car as I went by. I take it those two wonders have yet to show up."

Kit giggled, choked on her sandwich and had to wash it down with a swallow of milk. "No, they're not here yet."

Chuckling, Sally ambled in to see her patient. Kit followed, hesitating inside the hall doorway as Sally entered Clara's room. Her laugh ended abruptly. A few minutes later she came out of the room, white-lipped, with a strange look in her eyes.

"What is it?" Kit asked.

"I need to see Augusta." Leaving Kit out in the hallway, the nurse closeted herself with Kit's aunt. Left alone, stomach churning, Kit went to the dining room to wait for what seemed like hours before Sally and Augusta appeared.

One glance at her aunt's tear streaked face as Sally assisted her into a chair, and Kit knew something was terribly wrong. She gripped the back of the chair.

"Has Gramma gotten worse?"

Taking a long breath, Sally squared her shoulders. Kit got the impression this was a part of her job Sally had faced one too many times. "Dearie, your dear Gramma is gone."

"Gone?" Kit repeated the word dully. "Gone?"

Sally nodded. "She died quietly, in her sleep." Solicitously, she turned to Augusta. "Will you be okay?"

"If only I'd checked on her." Augusta hugged her arms to her chest. "I'm too late...again."

"Nonsense," assured the nurse. "There was absolutely nothing you could have done. She died in her own bed, just as she wished."

Their exchange whirled around Kit, but she scarcely took it in. Though she came to the city knowing her grandmother had little time left, the reality of her death left her shaken. If only she'd spent more time with her.

As if from a distance, Kit heard Sally call for an ambulance, then watched as white coated attendants rushed in and took away her grandmother's now still form. She sat, unmoving, as Sally helped Augusta out the door to her car. Neither spoke to Kit, nor asked her if she'd like to go along to see to these last details. She might as well have been invisible. Sally had enough to do taking care of her aunt without having to concern herself with another physically disabled individual.

"Disabled! Useless!" The words taunted Kit. She felt utterly helpless and utterly worthless. "Why did I even come here, Lord? I haven't helped and I may have made things worse, especially for Aunt Augusta." Slowly the tears gathered in Kit's eyes and splashed down her cheeks.

"Oh, God, now what? What do I do now?" Someone pounded on the front door, and Kit quickly brushed away her tears. Numbly she admitted Lars and Uncle Edmund, feeling nothing but loathing for these hulking predators who pushed past her into the house.

"What's for breakfast?"

"There isn't any!" snapped Kit. Without pause, she rasped, "Gramma Clara is dead."

Edmund put a hand against the wall to steady himself. With

a frightened look in his pale eyes, Edmund glanced toward the bedroom. "She's not still here?"

"No. They took her away a little while ago. Sally and Aunt Augusta are also gone."

Edmund slumped into his usual chair. With trembling fingers he caressed the hourglass, but didn't pick it up.

"Are you two going to the funeral home to help Aunt Augusta with arrangements? I'm sure she could use your support right now."

Edmund didn't answer. Kit didn't even think he heard her. Lars rolled his eyes. "Nothing's going to keep dear Augusta topside now. By tomorrow they'll have her tucked away in a nice, safe, rubber room."

Hardly able to contain her fury, Kit clenched her hands. She fled to the bedroom for Keith's card. Her hand shaking, Kit dialed the number. "Please, Lord. Please let me get hold of him."

"Hello." It was his sister's voice.

"Is Keith there?" She tried to keep her voice from trembling.

"Kit, is that you? No, I'm sorry. He left early this morning. Today's the last day of the conference. He wanted to attend a couple more workshops before heading for the amusement park with you and the girls. May I give him a message?"

Gripping the phone, Kit closed her eyes. "Just tell him I called," she whispered. "Gramma's dead." Hanging up the phone, she felt choked by an unseen menace stalking her. Sticking her head into the living room, she said, "I'm going for a walk. If you leave don't lock the front door."

She knew what she was doing was incredibly foolish, and knew she took a risk. But she had to escape the confines of that house. She had to get away to think. Desperately, she longed for Keith, longed for his comforting presence, and his calm, assuring words. At a time like this, she needed someone to wrap their arms around her. But just *someone* wouldn't do. She needed the tall, enigmatic man who'd stolen her heart in a matter of days. *Stolen her heart?* What was she thinking!

Surely she didn't love the man who brought her to Minneapolis only as a favor to her doctor? It wasn't possible. Love grew slowly over time. Love didn't burst forth, not like this...suddenly, and without warning. But it had. Somehow, her love for Keith had been growing since the first moment she met him in Dr. Ellis' office.

When all her doubts overwhelmed her, she discovered love. Not infatuation. This love grew stronger with each day, filled her inner being and warmed her clear to her toes. This was love. "I love him," she whispered in breathless awe at the strange, wonderful feelings unfurling inside like a precious blossom. Yes, she really and truly loved him. Regardless of whether or not he ever reciprocated her love...and she was certain he would not...she loved him.

"As I love you," whispered a small voice inside her mind.

Kit lifted her face to the cloudless sky. "I understand God. I understand! You love me! No matter what, you love me!" Her doubts evaporated with the understanding of God's sure love for her.

With that love came a surety of purpose. Kit knew that not only did she have a mystery to solve, but also, until she did, Augusta would never be safe.

Questions buzzed in her head. What should she do with the contents of the jewelry box? How did her aunt's "accidents" fit in with the whole picture? What *was* the whole picture? Frustrated, Kit bowed her head and committed the problem to her Heavenly Father. The love she had for Keith helped her, for the first time, to truly understand God's love for her.

Peace settled over her. "Thank you, Lord," she breathed. "Thank you." Turning around, Kit started back for the house.

Inside, the house seemed to echo its emptiness. Neither Lars nor Uncle Edmund sat in the living room. With a shrug, Kit checked the rooms. She hesitated outside her grandmother's bedroom. Gathering her courage, she glanced inside.

"Oh, no!" Kit's knees trembled at the chaos sprawled before her eyes. Everything had been thrown aside or torn asunder. China had been smashed, sheets slashed. As panic surged through her, Kit ran from the room.

Who had done this awful thing? Why had someone desecrated the room that so recently held her dear grandmother? Why? Kit shivered. Had someone been searching for the manuscripts? Or was this a random looting? After all, she *had* left the house unguarded.

Arms hugged to her chest, Kit slammed the door closed. Sucking in a breath to calm herself, she reached for the phone to alert the police. Hand poised over the phone, she stopped. What if a family member had done this? If only she could talk to Keith. She could probably have him paged at the conference, but shrank from the idea.

She looked up. "Lord, I know you love me. You said to trust you. Well, I need help now."

The phone under her hand trilled, making her jump. Heart pounding Kit picked it up. "Hello," she answered unsteadily.

"Kit, are you all right?"

Kit closed her eyes in gratitude. *Thank you Lord Jesus!* "Keith, thank goodness you called."

"What's wrong?" Keith felt her fear over the phone and he gripped it more tightly. "Kit, talk to me."

"Keith—" He heard her choke back a sob. "Gramma Clara's dead. She died during the night. After everything else, Aunt Augusta's fall, Lars and Edmund acting so strange...." Again the choked sob. "I couldn't stand staying here in the house alone with those two, so I went for a walk. I know I shouldn't have, but I had to get away and think."

He heard her shuddering breath and wanted nothing more than to hold her close. *"Lord, I want to hold her."* As he sent the prayer heavenward, all his "ideal wife" standards for the perfect wife shattered with the awareness they didn't matter. Maybe they never did. Keith didn't need a woman with a perfect body. He needed a woman who not only fit neatly in his arms, but who was also the other half of himself. He needed...*Kit!* The realization staggered him. And she needed him!

Her wavering voice brought his attention back to the matter at hand. "When I returned," she gulped audibly, "Gramma's bedroom had been all but destroyed."

"Kit, love. Are you alone?" Absently, he wiped his palm on his slacks.

"Yes, I'm here alone. Oh Keith, ever since I first arrived, there have been such weird things happening. I'm scared."

"Kit, hang on. I'll come as soon as I can get away. I have an appointment with someone in a few minutes. It's something I can't easily cancel."

"It's all right. I...I understand." She didn't fool Keith.

"Kit, are you certain no one is there?" What if the person who'd burglarized her grandmother's room was still in the house?

"Pretty sure. Just a minute, I'll check."

Hearing the clunk of the phone, Keith shouted, "Wait! Don't go off on your own!" Kit missed his warning. Guessing she was checking the house, he silently prayed for her safety.

He was sweating by the time she picked up the phone again. "Keith?"

"Don't you have more sense than that!" he exclaimed. "What if the burglar had been hiding in the house?"

"But I thought..." His anger seemed to bewilder Kit. "I...I didn't think."

She was very near the breaking point, and Keith forced himself to a calmness he didn't feel. "Kit, I want you to lock yourself in. Don't admit any strangers. Promise. I'll get away just as soon as I can."

"About the amusement park, I don't think..."

Keith cut off her apology. "That's not important. I called the girls and they already found another ride. If not for this unscheduled appointment...."

"Wait," said Kit. "I think I hear Sally and Aunt Augusta. I'll be all right now."

"Are you sure? I'll come as soon as I can get away, and that's a promise. But Kit, trust God. He *will* take care of you."

Reluctantly hanging up the phone, Keith pictured Kit's frightened face and groaned. He'd been so smug when he'd promised to watch out for her.

Though she had tried to control it, Keith heard her fright and it pained him.

Kit's dilemma on his mind, Keith gave scant heed to the colleague who accidentally bumped into him as he strode down the wide hallway. "'Scuse me," he murmured absently.

"It's all right. Dr. Long, isn't it?" The woman's smile invited further acquaintance.

Surveying the woman's lush figure, and knowing her to be bright, articulate and intelligent, Keith was surprised to realize he felt nothing for the lovely woman, nothing at all. With a grin, he acknowledged that his image of the "ideal woman" now meant a petite figure and wide blue eyes.

His face set, Keith determined to cut his obligations short and to go to her. A hand on his shoulder forestalled him.

"Dr. Long, good, you're still here. We have an emergency situation on our hands and we need your expertise. Now."

As Kit hung up the phone, Sally and Augusta returned. She heard the now familiar clump of crutches on the linoleum floor of the kitchen, and the more muffled clump on the rugs in the dining room. Sally took one look at Kit's face. "What's wrong?"

"Come and see." Kit led the way to her grandmother's bedroom. At least Sally couldn't say she was imagining things.

"Oh, oh, oh!" cried Augusta, clutching the crutch. "What next!"

"Dearie, what happened here?" The words appeared to be an accusation.

"Isn't it obvious? Someone searched Gramma's room. All I know is that I left Lars and Uncle Edmund here this morning to go for a walk. When I returned they were gone and I found the room like this."

Anger flashed in the nurse's usually placid face. "You left? Where did you go?"

"Out."

Augusta's eyes widened. "Why anything might have happened. I told you, Kit, you shouldn't go out alone."

"I know, Aunt Augusta. I'm sorry. I just felt I had to get away for awhile. I'm afraid I asked Lars not to lock the door, but I really didn't expect them to leave."

Her arms akimbo, Sally frowned at Kit. "Thanks to your thoughtlessness, dearie, a prowler was able to enter the house."

Miserably, Kit shook her head. Could *she* have caused this? Something didn't add up and she felt decidedly uneasy. Meeting the nurse's accusing gaze, she said slowly, "That doesn't make sense. If it was a burglar why didn't he take something valuable like one of the silver tea services, or the fine china cups or... It doesn't make sense at all." Kit stopped short of accusing Lars. He would delight in such destruction.

Augusta fought to regain some measure of composure. "Police. Shouldn't we call the police?"

Sally's eyes narrowed. "What good would that do? Whoever it was won't be back." She skewered Kit in her reproachful gaze. "No one will leave the door unlocked again. Right now, Augusta, what with your dear mother awaiting burial, police interference might delay things." She put a hand on the taller woman's trembling shoulder. "It might be a long time before you return to normal as it is."

"Are you sure? Of course, you're right. I could not bear any more. Not right now."

"Come Augusta, let me help you into the bedroom. I think you need to lie down. Don't you worry. Everything's going to be fine, just trust me."

Augusta straightened. "Oh no, not now. I have calls to make."

"Go ahead then." Picking up a rumpled blanket, Sally folded it. "But then you must lie down." She sighed. "I suppose I'd better straighten out this mess. By the way Augusta, you don't have anything of Clara's in your room, do you?"

"Not that I know of. You know how she wanted all her things around her." Sitting by the phone, Augusta picked up the receiver.

Kit watched Sally's broad back as she leaned over to strip the bed. "Sally, I'll help you clean up Gramma's room," she offered.

"Thanks, dearie, but I'd prefer to do it myself." Once such a simple statement would have filled Kit's mind with doubt about her worth, but not now. Now, thanks to Keith, she knew how much God valued her.

"I'll fix us a light lunch, then." In the kitchen Kit quickly fixed a simple lunch of roast beef sandwiches, carrot and celery sticks, leftover salad, milk and cookies.

Silence reigned at the table. The three might as well have been strangers for all the notice they took of one another. Sensing the women's condemnation, she sighed. Leaving the door unlocked *had* been a foolish thing to do.

Pushing back her plate, Sally picked up her cup. "Kit, I suppose you'll be making plans to return home soon." She paused a moment to freshen her tea before asking, "Did Clara ever tell you why she wanted you to come to Minneapolis?"

Kit swallowed the last bite of the melt-in-your-mouth Spritz cookie she'd been eating. "No, she never had the chance. Mostly she just reminisced about the past. She did say one strange thing though. Something like *varning*.

Augusta's head jerked up. "Are you certain you heard correctly, Katalina?"

"I think so. It means warning, doesn't it?"

Augusta turned her cup around and around in her hand. "Why should mother say such a thing to you?

Sally shrugged. "You mustn't put too much stock in it, Kit. Your grandmother was dying. Like as not her mind wandered a bit now and again."

Kit doubted that, but didn't contradict the nurse. Augusta slowly shook her head. "Wait a minute. Kit, Mother left something for you...a letter."

"She did?" Sally and Kit exclaimed together.

"Let me get it." Augusta reached for her crutches leaning against the wall.

Sally heaved herself to her feet. "No, Augusta, you stay put. I'll get it. Where is it?"

"*Tack a mycket.*" With a relieved sigh, Augusta explained where she'd kept the letter.

A moment or two later, Sally pushed a folded note into Kit's hands. "Read it," she commanded, easing her bulk onto a kitchen chair.

Biting her lip, Kit opened the note, stared at it a moment then handed it over to her aunt. "Please, it's in Swedish."

Augusta took the note. "Mother never did learn to write English well." Her hand shook as she read. "*Var snäll och—*"

"In English please, Aunt Augusta," Kit begged.

"*Ya*, of course." Augusta frowned as she skimmed the note. "It says, 'Please return music manuscripts to Sweden. They belong in a museum. Be careful. Warning. Love..." Puzzled, Augusta glanced up. "I don't understand. Obviously Sally, you're correct. Mother's mind must have wandered these last few days."

"May I have the note?" Kit took it. "It's Gramma's first...and last letter to me."

"Do you know what your grandmother meant?" Sally quizzed. "Maybe she was more alert than we know."

"I think she knew what she was talking about," Kit agreed. Folding the note, she tucked it into the pocket of her blouse. "I have an idea—" She stopped. She'd made a promise to Gramma Clara not to speak of the jewelry box. Did it still hold, even now after her death?

Besides, her troubles could be over. Gramma was gone. When she returned home, maybe Keith could help her figure out who to contact about the manuscripts. She decided to let the matter ride.

While Kit cleaned up the dishes, Sally settled Augusta down for a nap. As Kit hung up the dishtowel, like bad pennies, she heard Lars and Uncle Edmund pounding on the door. Reluctantly, she let them in. Without a word, Uncle Edmund slunk over to his chair and faded into its roomy interior. Lars ambled around the house as though he owned it, poked into drawers, lifted vases, and surveyed everything around him for all the world like an auctioneer deciding on the value of the merchandise.

His presence drove Kit into the bedroom where, with the aid of Sally's pills, her aunt slept. Kit opened her Bible but found herself unable to concentrate. From the other room, she heard the hum of low voices through the partially open door. Laying back on the bed Kit tried to rest, but sleep eluded her. How long before Keith arrived? Her heart thumped painfully at the very thought of him.

The oppressiveness of the day bore down on her full force. Kit felt the tension in the house and her peace ebbed away to uneasiness.

Suddenly Augusta's eyes flew open, and she stared wildly at Kit. "Oh, Kit! I understand my nightmare. I know who caused Father's death, and it is not my fault!"

CHAPTER THIRTEEN

Whose hatred is covered by deceit, wickedness shall be shewed before the whole congregation. Proverbs 26:26

Getting up, Kit closed the bedroom door. Her hands shaking with eagerness, Kit said more calmly than she felt, "Tell me, please."

"Oh, Kit." Augusta sat up and rubbed her damp forehead. "For so long I have been trying to hide. I was terrified of remembering what happened the night Father died. I was afraid of discovering I was even more guilty than I thought."

Slowly Augusta unlocked her tightly clasped hands. "You made me take another look at myself. I was so frightened when the nightmares started up again. I'm still frightened." She paused, then continued, her voice growing stronger and steadier as she spoke, "Maybe, I am going crazy, but I found out something very important. Kit, that night, Mother, Father and I were having a pleasant evening together when a knock sounded at the door."

A sad smile flitted across Augusta's thin face. "It was Uncle Edmund. Laughing, Mother hugged him and pulled him inside. She was so excited to see him."

"So your uncle did come to America before your father died."

"*Ya*, maybe that's one of the things which confused me. I believed he came later. I couldn't understand why he should sometimes appear in my nightmares. Now I know he *was* there. And he was very angry. He insisted Father turn something over to him...some papers of some kind." Augusta's brow creased in concentration.

Kit leaned forward eagerly. "Did he say what the papers were?"

"I don't recall. He just started screaming at Father. He said such awful things! Father yelled back. Then...then he clutched his chest. Motioning for me, he gasped, 'Get my pills, Gussy. Hurry!'"

Augusta's eyes shimmered with tears. "Father was the only one who ever called me Gussy."

Taking a long shuddering breath, Augusta continued, "By the time I returned just moments later," Augusta covered her face as tears streamed down her pale cheeks, "Father was...dead." She put down her head and wept tears she'd held back for forty years.

Kit put a hand on her aunt's arm until she calmed. "What happened then?"

"I...I'm not sure. I think I fainted. Father and I were very close. He was as much a friend as a father. And there he was on the floor, his hands still clutching his chest, but he wasn't breathing." Augusta gulped, her voice steadied. "By the time Uncle Edmund came to America legally the next year, I was just beginning to recover from my breakdown."

"Except you didn't really forget. The whole thing was just waiting to explode. If only you'd gotten all this out years ago."

Smiling shakily, Augusta reached for another handkerchief. "I should have done something about it, but I was afraid I'd go crazy again. Every time I'd mention having a dream of any kind, Uncle Edmund would look at me like..." Augusta shrugged.

"I'll bet he did," Kit said dryly. "As long as you didn't remember, he felt safe. Think about this. Your accidents started only after your nightmares returned."

Her aunt stared at her. "What?"

"They weren't accidents, Auntie. Someone deliberately tampered with the step and put a trip cord across the bathroom threshold. I don't know who, though Lars is a prime candidate in my book. I just don't know why he'd try to protect his father. There's certainly no love lost there!"

Augusta's eyes widened. "Kit, what will we do?"

"Don't tell anyone you know about Uncle Edmund and your father. Not yet. At least you know the truth, and you know you're not crazy."

"No, I'm not. I have been confused about things lately, but I am not confused about what happened that night." Augusta shook her head. "I've kept this inside too long. It's time I settle things with Uncle Edmund."

Kit cringed at the determination on her aunt's face. Augusta's indecisiveness was gone, but for both their sakes she needed to persuade her aunt to wait. "Auntie, it might be best if—"

Her aunt interrupted before Kit could finish. "That man practically destroyed my life with his continual hints at my sanity. I haven't known peace for forty years. I must, I *shall* confront him. Uncle Edmund was the one who coaxed Mother into sending me away. Now I know why." Her aunt faltered. A spasm of pain crossed her face.

"Are you all right?"

"Headache." Augusta's voice slurred.

Before Kit could respond, Sally stuck her head in the door. "Hungry? I have a light dinner prepared. I know it's early, but I thought you might be ready for a bite."

Augusta glanced in dismay from Kit's slacks to her own rumpled gown. "I guess it's too late to change for dinner." Standing up, she smoothed her dress before slipping her crutches under her arms.

Kit followed her aunt into the dining room and sat down across from Lars. When Augusta deliberately seated herself across from her uncle, Kit quailed. "Lord," she breathed softly. "It's in your hands. I'm trusting you to keep Augusta safe. Please work things out."

After grace was said, Augusta tried to get her uncle's attention but he ignored her. He kept his eyes on his plate as he shoveled food in his mouth. Lars, however, watched Augusta with a smirk on his lips. Catching his expression, Augusta seemed to shrink back into her chair. Her chin trembled.

She turned to the steady, reliable nurse for reassurance. Smiling, Sally passed over the meatballs swimming in mushroom sauce. "Did you sleep well, Augusta? I thought you might sleep longer."

"I slept well, thank you, Sally."

"And you, Kit, did you lay down as well?"

"I couldn't sleep." Involuntarily, she glanced toward her aunt.

Edmund glanced up at that moment as well. Rage burned in his pinched face. Lars, grinning silently to himself, gobbled up enormous amounts of food. When he did glance up, his cold scrutiny sent shivers down Kit's back.

She had come so far in the last few days, but now, unexpectedly, Lars' cold survey brought back all her doubts. She felt small, disabled, and helpless. She closed her eyes momentarily. Jesus help me, she cried silently.

The image of her unconditional love for Keith helped her focus on God's unconditional love for her. *"Thank you, Lord."*

Maybe Lars did make her feel like melting gelatin, and maybe she wasn't strong...but her Lord was. Somehow with God's help she would be strong for her aunt. The look on Augusta's face convinced her that her aunt's fear was not going to long deter her from facing her tormentor.

An uneasy silence reigned over the table, and Kit was relieved when Sally shooed them from the room so she could clean up. Until that moment, it hadn't occurred to Kit that Sally would soon have to look for another position. Kit thought it somewhat sad.

If Kit thought her aunt would meekly return to her room, she was mistaken. Augusta clumped into the living room after Lars and her uncle. She took Kit's usual place beside Uncle Edmund. From the wide doorway between the two rooms, Kit watched her aunt slump, then straighten her shoulders. Nervously, Augusta smoothed her skirt. "Uncle Edmund, were you in America before Father died?" Her first foray brought Edmund to the edge of his chair.

"You're sounding strange again, Augusta," he growled.

"I know you were."

Edmund's gaze snapped to Augusta's white, determined face. "How could you know that unless..." His voice shook. "Stop!"

Lars jerked to attention. Desperately afraid for her aunt, Kit prayed silently.

Years of pent up feelings of guilt, worthlessness, and doubt boiled out of her. Augusta refused to remain silent. "You were there. I know you were there, Uncle Edmund." Starting low, Augusta's voice grew louder as her accusations hit home.

Edmund stared at Augusta as though he'd never seen her before. Muttering thickly, he shrank under her accusations. "*Ya*, I vas there. I vas there."

"You murdered my father," Augusta accused him, her voice rising.

"Only vanted vhat vas mine." Edmund's brogue grew deeper with each syllable.

Lars put out a hand as though to still his father. Or was it Augusta he wished to silence? Kit stilled her own impulse to go to her aunt. There was nothing either Lars or Uncle Edmund could do while Sally was in the house. Her cheerful humming from the kitchen comforted Kit.

Augusta was not finished. "You wanted papers from Father. You accused him of stealing something from you. My father never stole anything in his whole life. He was the kindest, gentlest, most honest man I have ever known."

"I come for vhat vas mine, Clara. *Ya*, tell the old man. I vill have the papers. You understand. They are mine."

"Mother kept nothing which belonged to you." Augusta sucked in a deep breath.

"*Ya*, Clara, vhy you take them from me? Vhy did you leave me?"

"Gramma Clara, at least, never let a man burn to death," Kit blurted. She bit her lip, horrified at her slip.

Edmund's head jerked toward her. His gaze glittered with hate. "Kat. All your fault Kat. Vhy you come back to haunt me? The papers belonged to the old man. I worked and slaved for him. I took the papers. They belonged to me, *to me* you understand. I vill have them!"

"Murderer!" screamed Augusta, tears streaming down her face. "Murderer!" Slumping back into his chair, Edmund closed his eyes.

Rushing from the kitchen, Sally gathered the hysterical Augusta in her arms to calm her. Kit shivered under the cold glance Sally shot her as the nurse helped the sobbing woman to her room. "You've done it now," Sally muttered.

Doubts assailed her before Kit pushed them away. Yes her aunt was crying, but the hysterics were already dissipating. Augusta was not the same woman she was a few days ago. She was stronger. Deep inside, Kit felt an assurance her aunt would be all right.

Following Sally to the bedroom, Kit arrived in time to find her preparing a shot for her aunt. Startled, Sally stepped back at the interruption.

"Why does she need that?" Kit questioned.

Languidly Sally inserted the shot and watched it take affect as she soothed Augusta. "It'll be fine, Augusta. Soon everything will be fine."

As Augusta's eyes closed, Sally put the syringe in her little bag. "I gave her a tranquilizer. Maybe you could use one as well?"

Kit sat on her bed. "I don't need anything like that. But maybe I'll try to rest awhile."

Smiling compassionately, Sally patted Kit's pillow. "I'll look in on you later, dearie." She did, too. Several times. "Can't sleep yet? Well, keep trying."

While trying to rest, Kit reviewed the events of the past few days. She was certain the papers Edmund wanted were the same ones in the jewelry box. No wonder he'd never been able to find them.

Gramma Clara must have hidden them in the box for safekeeping before giving it to Sophia, who took it away. All those years, the papers weren't even in Clara's possession. But who knew, besides Gramma Clara herself?

Kit was thankful she hadn't told anyone about the papers. Who had removed the box from her suitcase and replaced it again? And why? Was it worth the risk to find out? Did it even matter any more now that her grandmother was gone? She'd tell Keith about the papers as soon as possible. Surely he'd help her find a way to return the valuable manuscripts to Sweden. Once everyone knew the manuscripts had been returned, her aunt, if she did know something, would truly be safe.

After about an hour, Kit restlessly got to her feet. Her aunt lay unmoving on her bed. Obviously she would not awaken for some time. Kit headed toward the living room. Sally sat near Edmund, conversing impatiently in low tones. She glanced up when Kit entered the room. "What are you smiling about dearie?"

"Soon I'm going home."

"Planning on taking Clara's inheritance with you, huh?" Lars sneered.

"No, I'm not!" Kit retorted. "I don't care if I get a thing!"

"Sure!" Lars snickered.

"Oh, hush, Lars," commanded Sally.

"All I vanted, was vhat vas mine," whined Edmund.

"Still want your papers, Father?" Lars stared at Kit. His lips curled in a chilling smile.

Sally smiled calmly at Kit. "Kit, Edmund wants his papers."

Kit froze. "What do you mean?"

Lars surveyed her coldly. "We know you have them stashed away somewhere."

The evil of the house closed in on her. It was Lars all along. He was the canker that ate away at the foundation of this home. She turned to Sally for help, but the compassionate nurse's visage had hardened. "Sally?"

"Dearie," Sally grated, "I know you have those papers hidden some place."

"Why do you think that?" Kit stalled, trying to understand.

"Don't forget, dearie, I heard your aunt read Clara's note to you."

Sally smiled a bone chilling, deadly smile. "Well, are you going to get them for us or do you want your things ripped up like Clara's?" Kit's stomach churned.

Realizing she'd been holding her breath, Kit let it out slowly. "So it wasn't a prowler, after all. I thought not. Lars did it, didn't he? You checked it again, didn't you Sally, when you cleaned up? You sure had me, had us all, fooled."

Sally's chins shook with repressed laughter. "No use stalling, dearie. Get the manuscripts. I've been waiting far too long. I'm not going to scrape and slave one more minute for you or your precious aunt."

At the unsympathetic look on her face, a look echoed on the faces of Lars and Edmund, Kit limped to the bedroom. Passing the phone she reached out a hand.

"I wouldn't if I were you," warned Lars from the doorway.

In the bedroom Augusta lay on the bed, her chest moving up and down slowly, her face drawn and bloodless. "Oh, Lord, what if it wasn't simply a tranquilizer?"

She lay a shaky hand on her aunt's neck. Though she didn't know how to take a pulse, she could feel faint movement under her fingers. At least her aunt was alive. "Help me, Lord. Protect Augusta."

She squared her shoulders. Though she couldn't run for help, there had to be another way. Biting her lip, she tried to think. Glancing at her watch, she was surprised to find it was nearly six o'clock. Surely Keith should be here by now. Where could he be?

Opening her suitcase, Kit pulled out the jewelry box. She tucked it under her arm and returned to the living room. Edmund saw the box first. "Kat, you still have the box. Why the box?" He reached out his arms and snatched it away from her. Mumbling softly to himself, he cradled it. "So that's where they've been all this time. In Kat's jewelry box, *ya*. Claus gave it to Clara on their wedding day. And she gave it to Sophia—"

"Is that why the old lady wanted you to come to Minneapolis?" Lars demanded.

"Gramma did ask me to bring it, though at the time I had no idea why. But tell me, why didn't you take them when you went through my luggage the other day?"

They all stared at her as though she'd lost her senses. Sally glanced at Lars who shrugged. "We didn't know you had them. We thought Clara gave them to you for safekeeping after you got here!"

"Someone took the box, then put it back."

"Not us," said Lars. Getting up he ripped the box from his father's grasp. "I want those papers. Where are they?"

He dumped the box in Kit's arms.

Slowly Kit lifted the lid. In her hand she held the file she'd picked up on the way out of the bedroom. "Sally, you're Augusta's friend, how did you get involved?"

"Oh, I was good enough to do their dirty work, but not good enough to marry into the family. Isn't that right, Edmund? You'd never marry me, because Clara didn't approve. She didn't approve of her brother marrying a mere servant."

Edmund fidgeted, and sunk further into the chair. "Needed a divorce. Clara didn't like divorce."

Working on the box, Kit shook her head sadly for the woman who had poisoned her own life by focusing on what she didn't have, instead of on what she did. Kit gulped. How easily this could have been her years down the road. "Thank you, Lord," she whispered. "Thank you for sending Keith to show me your love."

"How did you know about the papers?" Fiddling with the screw, Kit stalled as long as possible.

"Edmund told me. He'd given up looking for them years ago." Sally laughed, shaking her head. "But when Lars came back after Clara was laid up, he overheard us talking about them. He threatened Clara, but she wearied of him and said nothing. When you showed up, I knew Clara was up to something."

"I don't see the connection."

Sally's smile chilled her. "Who else could she trust? Certainly not that idiot of a daughter. That note to you cinched it. Unfortunately, you had already starting digging up the past. When Augusta started having her nightmares again, I knew I had to take action."

"So Augusta began having 'accidents.' Now what? Are you planning to kill her?"

When Sally sucked in a breath, Kit faced her. "What was in that shot you gave her?" she demanded.

"Never you mind, dearie. If she does wake up she'll be completely bats."

Since coming to the city, Kit had lived under the tension and fear of the unknown. Now that she understood the direction of the evil, she felt calm and clear-headed. She also sensed a strength and power outside her human frailty.

Lord help me... She knew her timing had to be just right. Slowly Kit drew out the screw. "Why try to hurt Augusta?"

"I figured Augusta knew about the manuscripts. If she remembered about her father," Sally continued casually, "she might remember those, too." Sally's face twisted into a travesty of her former good-humored smile. "But she didn't know anything about them at all."

Kit struggled to keep the pain of Sally's betrayal from her face. "How did Gramma Clara ever get a hold of such valuable papers in the first place?"

Suddenly Sally's face once more relaxed into a smile as she licked her wide lips. "Seems Edmund was really quite the scoundrel back in Sweden. Kept getting deeper and deeper in trouble. Why did you think Katalina never trusted him? While the army was stationed in Stockholm, dear Edmund stole the papers. He thought since they had belonged to A. L., he had a perfect right to them after the old man's untimely death. But before Edmund could sell them, Clara got hold of them."

Kit's anger flared. "Untimely because Uncle Edmund let the poor man burn to death." Edmund ducked his head. His hand froze on the hourglass.

"Doesn't make much difference now, dearie, does it." Sally paused. "Will you hurry and get those papers out?"

"I'm getting them," Kit snapped. "But they're old. You wouldn't want them to crumble now, would you?" Carefully she eased the false bottom out of the jewelry box. "So what happened?" she prompted.

"Clara discovered them. She knew who'd taken them. She planned on returning them until Edmund threatened to implicate her in the scheme. So Clara hid them from him until he could cool down and be sensible. By then he was stationed far away and Claus had come to Sweden. Clara married Claus, and years later returned to America. Edmund kept trying to find the papers. He even followed his sister to America. He was convinced Claus knew all about them, and hated the man for taking Kat, and his sister, away from him.

"Claus' death scared him and he was more careful after that. All these years he's been terrified that Augusta might remember. Unfortunately, he's been too cowardly to do anything but make vague threats." She held out her hand. "Hand those papers over, dearie, they belong to us now. We'll sell them and live like we deserve to live." When Kit hesitated, her eyes narrowed. "Hand them over, *now*."

Kit held them out, but kept hold of them. Sally snatched at them and Kit cautioned, "If you tear them, they'll be worthless."

When Sally hesitated, Kit edged toward the door.

"Give them to me!" Sally demanded again, her face purpling with rage.

Lars lurched to his feet menacingly. "Come near me and I'll rip them to shreds," warned Kit, edging ever closer to the entryway.

Sally's mouth twisted into a cruel smile. "Where do you think you'll go? Know what will happen if you step out into the streets at this time of night? Those papers, dearie."

"First you call an ambulance for Aunt Augusta...now."

Under Kit's watchful eye, Sally reluctantly made the call. Replacing the receiver she took a step toward Kit. "Now give them to me, you little idiot."

Again Kit took two small steps toward the door. As she put her hand on the knob, she noticed the sand in Edmund's hourglass had run out. So had her time.

She felt the knob turn under her hand, heard the door squeak.

"Grab her," Sally screeched. "She's trying to escape!"

Lars lunged toward her.

Kit fell.

Like Augusta, she had failed.

Far away she heard a door open, then darkness.

CHAPTER FOURTEEN

And call upon me in the day of trouble: I will deliver, thee, and thou shalt glorify me. Psalm 50:15

Kit awoke to find herself lying on the living room sofa. A faint rustle caught her attention. Keith leaned over her, his eyes dark with concern. "How are you feeling?" he asked.

Kit raised a shaking hand to touch her forehead. "I have a monster headache." Feeling the bandage on her head, she grimaced. "What happened? I remember Sally screaming and Lars coming after me...."

"You bashed your pretty head on the door." Keith stroked her hair softly.

"So that's what happened? Where is Aunt Augusta? Is she all right?" Kit tried to sit up, groaned and lay back.

"Shh," Keith soothed her. "The ambulance arrived in time. Don't worry; they have her under observation at the hospital." Keith nodded with satisfaction. "In fact, they got here right after I took out that bruiser who jumped you. I suppose the ten ton weight was the nurse I wasn't privileged to meet last time?"

Kit sighed. "But you got here in time. I knew you would. I don't know how, but I knew."

"When the police took those three prizes away, the nurse was cheerfully cursing one and all. Your cousin was offering to tell the officers anything they wanted; for a large sum of cash, of course."

"Of course." Kit clasped Keith's large hand. "You know, you were right. I just needed to trust God. My physical impairment didn't matter at all when I left things in His hands." She glanced away shyly.

"Oh Kit." As he spoke, she heard self-condemnation. "I'm sorry I didn't get here before I did. I had no idea you were in immediate danger! Even so, I meant to get here much earlier. I would have too, but I was counseling a woman on the verge of suicide. As if that didn't keep me long enough, the car I rented broke down. Thankfully I got here when I did." Keith tightened his hold on her hand.

"It's not your fault," Kit said. She added softly, "God took care of me, just as you said He would. I know now He loves me, no matter what." She blushed.

Trying to divert her mind from the brush of Keith's shirt against her arms, she asked, "What about Uncle Edmund?"

Keith shook his head. "Poor fellow. He was mumbling and babbling to himself. They took him away, too, but I doubt there'll be charges brought against him. I fear his mind is completely gone."

Kit shut her eyes. "That's what he tried to do to my aunt."

Keith sat down on the edge of the couch and drew her carefully into his embrace. "Feel up to telling me the whole story? All I've gotten are bits and pieces."

Heart pounding, Kit could think of nothing but her love for the large, gentle man. As his warmth surrounded her, her mind cleared. Slowly she began to explain, then stopped. "I think I figured out who took the box. Gramma must have had Aunt

Augusta get it out to make sure of the papers. I'm convinced she wanted me to return them after she was gone. She just never got the chance to explain." Kit stared up at Keith. "The manuscripts! Where are they!"

"On the table. You dropped them when Lars went after you. What happened?"

"It all started in Sweden over forty years ago..."

A frown deepened Keith's face as Kit related the story, her involvement, and her attempts to get at the truth. "Why didn't you tell me all this?" he demanded. "I would never have left you here! I knew things weren't right, but I had no idea. Beth would have welcomed you."

"I couldn't leave Aunt Augusta. After all, she was the one in danger. Besides, I would just have been in the way at your sister's house."

A laconic smile spread across Keith's face. "I called her while you were, ah, out. And that's where you're going, just as soon as I help you pack. Beth is expecting us. She's horrified at the danger you were in, and so am I."

"But I'll be perfectly safe here now," argued Kit. Actually, she really didn't relish spending one more minute alone in the house.

"Sorry, Kit, but I say you're going with me," Keith said. "Even if I have to carry you."

Kit's eyes glinted a challenge. "Why must I obey you, Dr. Long?"

"Because that's what I expect of my future wife."

Kit gasped.

To Keith's consternation, her eyes filled with tears. "Pl...please don't tease me like tha...that," she stammered.

"Oh, Kit," Keith wrapped both arms around her and held her close. "Why do you think I'm teasing?"

Kit wiping tears from her cheeks. "Because I'm...I'm what I

am." She held up her hands for emphasis. "You don't want someone like me for your *wife!*"

"Silly little woman. I thought you were over all that nonsense about not being good enough. I love you, Kit. I don't care a fig about your disabilities." Leaning back, he surveyed her until she blushed. "You're a lovely, intelligent woman and I love you." Pausing, he lifted her trembling hands to his lips. "Hands and all."

Kit stared at him in amazement. Letting go of her hands, he held her close once more as his lips gently found hers in a kiss full of promise and love. "Can you possibly love this arrogant counselor, Kit?"

Tears of happiness sparkled in Kit's eyes. "I do, I already do!" She sniffed. "But about that obey part...."

"In the Lord. Only in the Lord, darling."

Kit sighed dramatically. "Surely you don't want a doormat."

"Perish the thought." He sighed, but his eyes lit with humor. "You know, Katalina Anderson, I had my wife all planned out. What she would look like, how she would act, how she would dress." He leaned his forehead against hers. "Then you came along and spoiled it all."

Kit made a face, then murmured softly against his suit jacket, "Yeah, well ever since I met you in Ken's office, you've played havoc with my thoughts, and you stole my heart. God showed me His love through you." She paused. "It seems like a dream."

"It's not, it's God."

Kit sat up again. "Gramma. The funeral, the papers. There's so much to do."

"You leave all that to me, Kit. When the funeral is over, love, we're going back to Kearney...together."

"Of course." Kit was puzzled. "That's the way we came."

Keith kissed her until the room spun. "Kit, do you mind a small wedding at Beth's church with just her family and us in attendance?"

"What! Wedding?" Kit breathed. "If I'm dreaming, I hope I never wake up. You're sure it doesn't matter?"

"No. Nothing matters except I love you, Kit, and you're going to be mine."

As he kissed her again, Kit knew her disability really didn't matter to him. *"Thank you God,"* she prayed silently. *"Thank you for helping me be strong enough to trust you."*

EPILOGUE

Through the window of the luxurious jet, Kit stared down at the ocean stretching out below in undulating waves. Feeling slightly queasy, she glanced toward her new husband and found his gaze upon her.

The look in his eyes brought a blush to her cheeks. "It was nice of your sister to invite Aunt Augusta to spend some time with her family. It'll give her time to completely recover before she returns home for good."

"Beth didn't want you to worry." Keith tugged a lock of her hair. "Besides, they really took to each other. Now stop worrying."

Kit let out a frustrated sigh. After all that had happened, she still felt jumpy. "Keith, are you sure the manuscript pages are safe?"

Caressing her cheek, he smiled. "For the hundredth time, yes. In less than twenty minutes we'll touch down in Stockholm and be whisked to the museum in a big black limo. The directors are as anxious to have those manuscripts as you are to return them. An all expense paid honeymoon isn't a bad deal for them, thanks to the insistence of the museum board."

She shivered at the deep tone in his voice as he continued, "Once we hand over the manuscripts, it'll be just you and me...together."

With a sigh of contentment, Kit snuggled closer to Keith. What a wonderful word, *together*.

~THE END~

About the Author

Carolyn R. Schiedies' credits include 12 novels, two novellas, a devotional journal, three poetry booklets, and contributions to several non-fiction books. She's written for a variety of publications, and has a regular column in a regional paper. Scheidies speaks to different groups on a variety of subjects, leads workshops on writing, and guest lectures at UNK. Visit her at http://welcome.to/crscheidies.